A COMPANION STORY TO ISOLDESSE

THE RED-UMBER FOREST

A NOVELLA BY

KIMBERLY GRYMES

TRACTOR BEAM PUBLISHING

ISBN-13: 978-1736179-38 (Paperback)
ASIN: B098WXN7MV (eBook)

Tractor Beam Publishing
P.O. Box 261, Rose Hill, KS 67133

www.kimberlygrymes.com

ANUMEN
TERMINOLOGY

Adamant – Official title of the overseer in a village or a grandburg.

Amula – (ah-mew-lah) Incantations that involve speaking certain words of the Anumen language that are encoded with instructions to manipulate the energy of the Eilimintachs.

Anumen – (ah-new-men) A race of beings that live on a world called Anuminis. The women of this species have a magical connection to the Eilimintachs.

Anuminis – (ah-new-min-is) The home world of the Anumens.

Arcstone – A powerful stone mined from the Black Mountain region on Anuminis. It has the capability of holding the essence of a single Anumen woman after her physical life ends. The arcstone can also form a permanent bond, a connection, to a living person, who can then see and hear the Anumen occupying the stone as well as utilize the magic of the arcstone.

Bearer mark – The outline of a crescent shape permanently inked on Anumen girls when they transition into their youthen years. The crescent shape symbolizes the ability to bear youthlings.

Creator mark – The outline of a full circle permanently inked on Anumen girls when they transition into their youthen years. The full circle symbolizes the ability to create and carry the seeds for life inside their body until needed. Once a season, a Healer will collect seeds from Creators, depending on how many Bearers are ready to bear youthlings. The seeds also provide a strong connection to the Eilimintachs, thus making Creators more powerful when casting amulas.

Daramum – means *grandmother*

Darayouthen – means *grandchildren / grandchild*

Eilimintachs – (el-im-in-tocks) Believed by the Anumens to be powerful beings with a connection to the elements who have blessed Anumen women with the ability to cast amulas.

Grandburg – Is the name for a large scale community comparable to a city.

Ittums – (it-tums) A green flower found on the leaves of an Ittum tree. When picked, the petals of the flower turn a bright yellow color.

Iya – means *hello* and *goodbye*

Prinor Family – The ruling family of Anuminis. The Adamants oversee the villages and grandburgs within each of the eight regions, and the Prinors oversee everyone, making the large scale decisions.

Sèara – (say-era) A powerful Anumen who can sense amulas, communicate with Anumens in the Unforeseen World, and sometimes get glimpses or premonitions through visions or dreams.

Sparren – A small bird, found in the Red Umber Forest region.

Transessent stone – A powerful white stone mined in the Black Mountain region on Anuminis. Anumen women use the stones to amplify their amulas.

The Unforeseen World – The place where an Anumen's essence ascends to after their physical life is over, and where they live out their second life before final rest.

Youthen – An Anumen term for a young child in their preadolescent years.

Youthling – An Anumen term for a young child prior to their youthen years.

1

I won't let her win. Not again. My sister and I have run this path along the river hundreds of times, and every time she's beaten me to the bridge.

"Come on, Uie," Issie shouts between huffs, her arms pumping at her sides.

"Stop calling me that."

She shoves her shoulder into mine, laughing. "Oh, you love it!"

Actually, ever since my best friend, Jasper, started using it, I don't mind it so much. But I'd never tell her that.

Sunshine peeks through the trees as we race along the river. I'm surprised Mum let us off from our chores so early in the day, but then again it was Isoldesse who asked. When has she ever said *no* to her prize child?

We round the bend and shoot out from within the forest. The narrow clearing snakes beside the river, leading us to the finish line: the stone bridge. The rapids off to my right are mild today, and I pretend the cascading water splashing along the rocks is a group of spectators cheering me on, pushing me to run faster—to win. Inside my chest, my lungs burn with each gasp of air, but I don't stop. Never has one of our races been this close before.

Issie's breathing is in sync with mine. Usually, during our races, she wears a taunting smile—always knowing she's going to win—but not today. I sneak a glance at my sister, whose cheeks are flushed behind the strands of black hair that have slipped free from her braid. Issie shoots me a wild look, and she shrills with frustration as I push ahead. That's when I know I've got her. I'm going to win.

She catches up, but barely. We're so close my hand smacks her hand, and she cries out, "Stop hitting me, Ulissa!"

"Well, don't run so close!"

One foot in front of the other, I push ahead again. I'm pounding wet grass beneath the new boots Daramum gave me. I'm convinced they are enchanted with good luck. They have to be. I've never been able to keep up with my little sister before, yet here I am, an arm's length ahead of her—the fastest youthen in our village.

I huff out a winded laugh. My feet are moving faster than ever before. It has to be the boots. Daramum's gifts are always special, not to mention I love the stories that accompany them. She's traveled every part of the eight regions from quaint villages to congested grandburgs.

The stone bridge is still a ways away, and amid our race, I imagine the story behind my boots. I picture Daramum buying them from somewhere in the Black Mountain region, the second most mystical place on Anuminis. She's told us many tales of her visits to the Black Mountain quarries where powerful stones like the arcstone and transessent stones are mined. I imagine the origin of my lucky boots begins somewhere deep within the caves, beneath the mountain where sunlight never touches, a miner plucks a powerful stone free from the roots of the mountain. He then grinds the stone into a fine shimmering powder before taking it to the nearest grandburg, where he barters it away to a local boot maker. The boot maker casts a bonding amula, fusing the enchanted powder to the leather used to make my beautiful boots, thus empowering them with good luck.

I'm probably wrong, and my boots are just boots. But if I finally beat Issie at a race, then maybe, just maybe, they do possess a hint of enchantment.

Lost in my thoughts, I misstep in the wet grass trailing the embankment. My right foot slips from the edge and I stumble toward the river. There's nothing graceful about my descent. Arms flailing and feet dancing about, I try to find traction along the slope of the sandy embankment.

Maybe my boots are not so lucky after all.

I continue, stumbling forward, and for a split second I think I've got my footing under control, but because I'm my dah's daughter, and my brain and body don't always work at the same time, my upper body teeters out over the water. Instinctively, my right foot stretches out and plunges into the shallows of the river while my left drags along the sand. Panic quickly fills me as icy cold water gushes against my leg, spilling over the top of the leather boot. I shriek and the sound echoes up and over the river and into the Red Umber Forest, disturbing a flock of sparrens nesting in the treetops. They take flight, creating a shadow as big as a storm cloud, momentarily shading me from the midday sun.

The panic swelling inside me isn't because I'm sad or even mad that I've ruined one of my brand-new boots. No. The fear that consumes me comes from how Mum will react when she sees what I've done. I should be used to the disappointed looks she's constantly giving me, yet each scowl—each shake of her head—crushes me more inside every day.

Even before we get to the stone bridge, the race is over, and I've lost once again.

2

My sister continues running our race, never stopping or noticing my absence.

"Issie, help me!" I yell. My toes are squished against a drenched sole. When I try tugging my leg free, nothing happens. The boot is firmly planted deep in the riverbed's mud.

When Isoldesse finally slows her pace, she's breathing hard. Then, with one hand shielding her eyes from the sun, she turns to look for me and missteps along the grassy ledge. I can't help but yelp as her feet stumble over the cliff-like ledge—a much steeper ledge than the one I stumbled down. My adrenaline is bursting beneath my skin as I watch, helpless and stuck. Though, I don't know why I exhaust my nerves when it comes to Issie. It's a pointless endeavor. I should know better. Mum's always saying how I spend too much time worrying and thinking when I should just react and do what needs to be done—like Issie.

Mid-fall, without hesitation, Issie raises her hands in front of her and shouts, *"Teacht gohaf luhte balla."*

Ignoring my drenched foot, I mutter the ancient words that command the Eilimintachs as if I were interpreting an amula for my teacher at school. "Come air… Make… Uh, make a wall. Some kind of wall. Oh, mudals! I can't even remember what *luhte* is for?"

The air in front of Isoldesse spins fiercely into a large disc before solidifying into a soft barrier. Her body lands against the invisible surface, which catches her seconds before she plunges face-first into the river.

"Did you see me?" Issie yells while bouncing and laughing on the invisible barrier of air.

Yeah, yeah. I saw you.

With a large push, she rolls onto her side. "We should jump off the ledge more often!"

"Uh, I don't think Mum would want us doing that on purpose. Even though it was pretty amazing!" I've become a bit of an expert in showering one with praise, especially if I know I'm going to need someone's help, and I'm definitely going to need Issie's help. She can be a bit carefree, but it's not completely her fault. Mum lets her get away with everything, and the stuff she gets in trouble for… Well, let's just say Mum finds some way to blame me. It's this ridiculous routine our family has fallen into.

But since Mum's not here, I can speak freely. "Let's not push our luck, okay. Besides, I need your help over here."

"I know. I'm just having a bit of fun!" Issie continues to flop around like a fish out of water. She's having fun, while I can barely feel my toes.

"Hey! Are you going to help me or not?"

"All right!" She presses her hands flat to the barrier. Normally, when casting an amula it doesn't matter how soft or loud you speak the ancient words. But because my sister is Little Miss Know-It-All and likes to rub it in my face, she recites her amula loud enough for me to hear. "*Ompar mise nos.*"

Slowly, the barrier rises, lifting Issie until she's level with the grassy ledge.

Show-off. Holding my tongue, I silently tell myself to be nice. If anyone can get me out of this mess, it's my sister.

Now safely on the ledge, Issie lifts her hands and shouts, "*Déanta!*" The air within the barrier wavers and slowly dissipates until there's nothing left but the memory of its existence. She jogs over, a smug grin forming between two rosy cheeks. "Mum's going to be livid when she sees you've ruined your new boots." Her snickering doesn't help my mood.

"I know," I grumble. "Can you come down here? My foot is stuck." I yank my leg to show her. The motion only causes my boot to sink farther into the river's muddy bed.

Issie hops off the bank and shuffles sideways along the wet sand. When she reaches the bottom, she struggles to stop and slams into me.

"Whoa!" I yell. My body tilts out toward the river. I prepare myself for a swim, but Issie grabs my arm and pulls me up, away from the water's surface.

"Whoops, sorry."

"Yeah, well, help me up." With her arms looping beneath mine, we shift our weight away from the river, heaving until my leg and boot are free. We climb our way to the grassy path, putting distance between us and the embankment.

I lean against a tree on the edge of the forest. "Thank you."

"You don't have to thank me. You're still in a heap of trouble. Mum will not be happy when she sees this." Isoldesse grabs the boot and pours out the remaining river water.

Using the tree for balance, I snatch the boot from her, the leather squishing between my fingers. "You're telling me stuff I already know. How about you help me dry it?"

Ignoring my request, she leans back on her heels and points to her worn boots. "If I'd fallen in with these old things, Mum wouldn't have cared. But if I'd worn the boots Daramum had just given me… Well—"

"Issie, I know!" I don't mean for my tone to sound harsh, but my patience is wearing thin. I turn the boot over. The leather folds lining the top part of the boot are discolored from its original sandy brown.

Ruined. Completely ruined. Daramum will be so disappointed in me.

Issie stands nearby, brushing back the damp black strands of hair framing her face. She tucks them behind her ears and says, "You know Mum's not going to let you out of the house tonight, right?"

Oh, I'd almost forgotten about the show later this evening! Tonight the Prinor family is visiting our village, and they're bringing Fawness with them. Her name is Basira, and she's the current Fawness. The most powerful Anumens on Anuminis. She's a direct descendant of Fawn, the first woman blessed by the Eilimintachs with the power to cast amulas. I was taught in school that the Fawness' bloodline is the only bloodline with a direct connection to the Eilimintachs.

I've only glimpsed our Fawness once. A long time ago. But now she's coming here—tonight—to take the stage at our village's amphitheater and tell us one of her infamous stories. It's all the entire village has talked about for weeks.

Scratching at a loose piece of red bark from the tree I'm leaning on, I tell Issie, "I don't want to miss out on seeing Fawness. It's not fair that you got to see her last year." I glance up through the leaves, squinting at the sun, waiting for her to respond. When she doesn't, I say, "The Prinor family never comes to our village on their way south before the icy months. It makes me mad that Mum knew they would be staying up in Umberwood last year and took you."

"Yeah, well, Umberwood isn't anything special."

"I wouldn't know. You've seen more grandburgs than I'll ever see."

Mum started taking Issie on more of her trips once she became a youthen. Not quite an adult, but more responsible than a youthling.

"Trust me, Uie, you're not missing anything."

"Says the one who has seen one of Fawness's shows." I'd continue speaking my mind, which I rarely get to do, but Issie is distracted with fixing her hair. She's retied the end of her braid, which makes me think of what my braid must look like.

I do plan to see Fawness's show tonight. Ever since Gunrthii, our village Adamant, informed our village of tonight's special occasion, I've taken extra precautions to stay on Mum's good side. Helping her on the farm with more than just my usual chores, staying out of sight whenever she's in a foul mood, answering every question with an answer that will please her, even if it means lying. I don't want to give her any reason to keep me from attending tonight's show.

"Can you do something?" I hate asking Issie for help, but sometimes dire circumstances require unfavorable actions. "Don't you know an amula that will dry it? Please. You know Mum will force me to stay home tonight if she sees this!"

"Yes, she definitely will," she says, again not holding back her amusement.

"It's not funny, Issie! You and Mum travel to the capital and meet with the Prinor family all the time. You get to see the world and— Fawness! While Dah and I—"

Issie's expression hardens. "You think I like when Mum drags me off to the capital? To act as if I support her trying to convince the Prinors to bring back the Old World ways?" Her seriousness makes her look older, and her dark eyes tense like Mum's do right before she gives me one of her *do you realize what you've done* lectures. She jabs a finger into my shoulder. "You think I enjoy her constant watch over everything I do?" Issie's shoulders relax and her head sinks. "It's exhausting, Uie."

I didn't mean to upset her. I honestly thought she enjoyed going with Mum. I let the soaked boot fall from my fingers. It lands in a pile of fallen umber tree leaves. Before she walks away, I pull Issie in for a hug. "I didn't know."

"How could you? And why would I burden you with my stress when you've got plenty of your own?" Issie pulls away from my embrace. "I can't even imagine how you go on, day after day, with her constantly scrutinizing and bullying you."

I smirk, but only because I've grown used to hiding my true emotions on the subject. "She's our mum, and this is our life."

"Will we ever be free?"

"I don't know." And it's true, I don't. I know it's custom to marry and start a family, but I don't ever plan on leaving our village, and I highly doubt Mum will either. So, it seems we'll always be in each other's lives. Mum may want to bring back the Old World ways, but she'll never be granted permission to actually seek out and bring back technology. There's too much risk for a second Era of Chaos.

"*Magic and technology don't mix well,*" Dah would always remind Issie and me whenever Mum wasn't around. "*A darkness takes over. A greed for more.*"

Whenever we'd asked what he'd meant by *more*, he'd only say, "*Of everything. Influential Anumens in high positions in society, both men and women, were constantly seeking out* more *regardless of the consequences. It was a terrible time for our ancestors.*"

We're taught early in school about the Era of Chaos, a fifty-year-long period where Anumens feuded over how everyone should live. All we know for sure is that in the end, technology was banished. Something that infuriates Mum. She's a firm believer that we can coexist with both technology and amulas.

"I believe you, dear sister, are destined for great things. You will be free one day," I tell her.

Issie smiles with a sniffle. I should've known better than to assume she agrees with Mum's ideas. She's simply better at playing the *stay on Mum's good side* game.

She drops her hands from my shoulders and wipes her cheeks dry before telling me, "I will only ever be free if I know you're happy."

I don't want to dwell anymore on the parts of our lives we can't control, so I pick up my boot and inspect it. Issie steps to my side, staring into the forest behind me. After a few seconds, she wanders out between the trees, turning her head left and right as if she's looking for something. She disappears behind a wide trunk that's four times her size. When she emerges, she tells me, "You know you can leave, right? Maybe not today or anytime soon, but one day you can get married and raise a family far from here. No one is forcing you to stay in the village. Not even Mum."

I can't feel the crescent mark permanently inked between my shoulder blades, but the fact that it's there means I will have a family of my own one day. Unlike Issie, who bears the full-moon mark.

"I know," I tell her, shifting my weight against the tree. She brushes fallen leaves with her feet, searching behind the trees. "What are you looking for?"

She ignores my question and asks, "You wouldn't be wanting to stay for a boy, now, would you?"

My sister loves a good rumor. She and her friends are good at getting into everyone's business. The last thing I need is for her to whisper details about my life to the village, especially when it involves matters of the heart.

"I'm not sure what you mean," I lie. The topic of me and Jasper, whom I've been close friends with since we were youthlings, is not something I intend to discuss… out loud… with Issie. "Can we focus on my boot, please?"

"Only if you admit you like Jasper."

"Issie, we're just friends."

"Uie, I'm not helping you unless you—"

"Fine!" I tilt my head up to the sky and run my fingers along my braid, which is thick enough to prevent the rough edges of the tree trunk from poking my skull. I hate that I'm conceding to Issie's assumptions and pray to the Eilimintachs that she can hold her tongue around others. I puff out an exasperated breath and nod. "Yes. I have been considering Jasper to be more than a friend, but…" I pause, pushing forward on one foot while the other rests against the tree behind me. "…my feelings on the matter are not public. So, please, Issie, keep this between you and me."

Issie points a long stick at me and smiles. "I *knew* it!" She tosses it into a nearby bush, then bounces toward me and boops me on the nose. "You two are perfect for each other! Plus, he's probably the only other Anumen who understands what life is like in our home. He knows the real you, not the you that puts on a fake smile and hides your pain from everyone else in the village."

I have no words. My fingers are twiddling, twisting the bottom of my shirt, because she's right. Jasper understands what life is like under our roof. He always listens when I need to vent, sits close and lends me his shoulder when I need to cry, or offers a forest adventure to help distract me from the troubles I often carry.

Not wanting to talk about Jasper anymore, I ask, "What about you? Where do you see yourself when it's time to leave home?" The moment the question leaves my lips, I feel a twinge of guilt. I mean, Issie may find love one day, but she can never have youthlings of her own. Adoption is always an option, if there are youthlings or youthens who need a family, but our world has never had many orphans. It's custom for blood to remain with blood. There have been many nights I've lain awake wishing Mum would send me to live with Dah's sister, even if it is in the Black Mountain region. I'd miss Dah, and maybe Issie, and most definitely Jasper, but to wake up each day without the worry of what awaits me outside my bedroom door *is* tempting.

I glance at Issie, who has twisted her lips into a sour pucker. "I-I didn't mean to bring up—"

"No, it's okay," Issie says with a shrug. "I plan to apply for an apprenticeship here in the village, at our school. I'd love to spend my days teaching amulas to youthens, maybe even dabble with helping the Adamant with his responsibilities of overseeing our village."

"Ah." I laugh playfully. "An educator I can see, but I never knew you were interested in politics."

"I can't help it. I'm our mum's daughter. I have ideas and I want others to see value in those ideas."

"Quite the ambition, and yes, I'd say you're definitely more Mum than Dah. I'm sure Gunthrii will be as pleased to have your advice as he is with Mum's advice."

We can't help but laugh, knowing that it's a curse more than a blessing to share similarities with Mum. Issie makes her way over to me and takes my boot. She waves for me to follow. "Come on. I found a stump we can use to dry it on. Afterward, we can go home, eat dinner, and then *both* attend tonight's show."

3

BYE-BYE BOOT

I hop on one foot while using the trees for balance as I follow my sister deeper into the woods. The reddish-brown bark pokes at my palms with each landing and push-off. When I reach the oversized tree, I round it until I spot Issie in a small clearing with a stump in the center. The stump looks freshly cut with splinters spiking the edges.

"Did you think of an amula you could use?"

Issie blinks and nods. "*We* can use an air-current amula," she says, pointing a finger back and forth between us. She drops the wet boot in the center of the stump. "I'll start us off and then you can jump in and help."

"You want *me* to cast with you? But you're the more powerful Anumen."

Isoldesse positions her feet shoulder-width apart and raises one hand over her head, the other out toward my boot. "Yes, *we*. Now come on. Get into position."

I move in closer, clearing some fallen leaves with my bare foot until the forest ground appears. On my toes, I center my body and hold out my hands, waiting for her instructions. "Okay, ready."

She nods and begins the incantation, "*Teacht teas gohaf ag tirym.*" The leaves in the trees above rustle and a current of air streams toward us. A faint, semitranslucent shimmer of light glints within the stream of air as it circles her. With one hand still raised high, she uses her other to redirect the air flow toward the boot. It jostles a bit but doesn't fall from the stump.

"That's amazing," I whisper as the air flows around it.

I could never match her strength and expertise. It isn't in me. Literally. Issie is a Creator, and I am a Bearer. A Creator creates and carries the seeds for life inside their body. Once a season, the local healer will collect seeds from Creators depending on how many are needed. The Healer will then distribute the seeds to Bearers that are ready to have youthlings. Though Issie will never have youthlings of her own, as a Creator the seeds she carries intensify her amula abilities. The seeds are the source of our connection to the mystical Eilimintachs.

I used to hate that she was born a Creator. Night after night, while lying in bed, I used to think how if I'd been born a Creator like Issie, then maybe Mum would see me as an equal. But now, my heart aches knowing that my sister may never be a mum.

"Well, what are you waiting for?" Issie asks with a scowl.

She never specifically told me which amula to use.

Okay-okay. I can do this. I'll never be able to invoke a powerful amula like air manipulation. My air amulas are smaller—way, way smaller—like miniature whirlwinds to cool my stew.

Mudals! Uh, let's see.

Eyes wide, Issie gives me that *hurry up* look. I'm about to give up and just ask her to tell me what to say when I remember something I saw the other day. After class, I spotted some powerful amulas listed in a journal left open on my teacher's desk. One of them was water manipulation. While my teacher spoke with another student, I browsed the open pages, curious about the phrases and images scrawled inside.

I send a quick, silent prayer to the Eilimintachs that my memory won't fail me.

I can do this.

I hold my palm facing out toward the boot, while my other hovers high over it. Then, I pinch my fingers together and raise my hand up, ready to say the words and draw the water out and up into the air. I repeat this motion a few more times before taking a deep breath and saying, "*Tarach amach et tiin.*"

"No!" my sister yells, her eyes opening to their fullest just as a bright orange spark ignites within the current of air flowing past her hands. She immediately rolls her wrists and swings her arms up, redirecting the stream of fire toward the sky. A flock of sparrens take flight, their black wings are frantically flapping as they chaotically flee from the unintended ambush.

Issie and I stare until the last flickering red flame has vanished over our heads.

"Oh, Uie." Her voice is soft and concerned.

I lower my gaze from the sky to the stump where my boot sits, engulfed in flames.

4

AN INVITATION

After Issie extinguishes the fire, we bury the scorched boot and head home.

We walk in silence along the grassy path, following the curves of the river. I try to keep a steady pace, but with only one boot on, I struggle to keep up. The afternoon sun has begun its descent behind the trees. Before long, it'll be dusk and time to make our way to the amphitheater. That's if Mum lets me go.

Breaking the silence, Issie throws a stone into the river. "So, for next time, *tiin* calls the Eilimintachs to bring fire. The amula you saw should've been written with *ucea*, for water." She moves closer to my side and nudges me. "Her error, not yours."

I try to muster a smile as thanks, even though I'm fairly sure it was my error and not the teacher's. Casting amulas is everything to Issie, but not so much to me. I do enjoy it, but only when I have to. I can create light to illuminate our lamps or guide me if walking home after dark. I can embed a message into a leaf and send it to its recipient, but only a short distance. Nothing beyond our village. More complicated tasks like heating my bathwater, igniting a fire in the stove or fireplace, or creating air barriers for whenever I take a tumble are still left to Mum and Issie. But it's been years since Mum has caught me with an air barrier. Now, she lets me fall.

I can only imagine what sort of reaction Mum will have when she learns of my charred boot. I guess I should be happy that things didn't end worse than they did. I can't even fathom what Mum would do to me if Issie had gotten burned.

"What if you sneak in through our bedroom window and change into your forest boots while I distract Mum?"

"You want to help me hide this from her?" This is a first. Issie and I are close, but she's never offered to lie for me before. I brush my hands along my shorts, grabbing them and twisting the fabric nervously between my fingers. "She'll know. She always knows when I'm lying to her."

"Maybe you should stop lying to her then."

"You think I want to—" I stop myself before I say something I can't take back. I'm on the brink of tears and too tired to argue. "I appreciate what you're doing, but I messed up again. You'll just have to come back and reenact Fawness's story for me."

"Uie, I'm not going without you."

"No, really. It's okay. I mean, of course I want to go, but there's no point in us both missing out on tonight's show." I don't want to add the part about how I doubt Mum would keep Issie from attending, even if she caught her in a lie. But me, Mum won't hesitate to send me to my room and lock me in with one of her confinement amulas.

All thoughts of Mum and what she'll do to me later vanish when I hear whistling from within the forest ahead. The path curves away from us, so I can't see who's coming, but whoever it is will appear soon enough. I quickly half hop and half scurry over to the edge of the path, searching out the tallest section of grass. I position myself behind the greenish-yellow stalks, hoping to avoid the inevitable question of why

I'm only wearing one boot. Something that would most likely be brought up in their next conversation with my mum.

Isoldesse saunters past me, farther down the path, kicking rocks and grumbling, "At this pace it'll be dark by the time we get home."

"You don't have to wait for me. You can always run ahead. I'll be fine." I gesture to the path.

"Yeah, right! Mum told us to stay together. She'll be livid if I show up without you."

I wonder how much Issie believes Mum would—no, *could*—be upset with her? Maybe Mum expresses her anger or disappointment in another way with Issie's mishaps. If so, her disappointment never shows in the presence of others.

"It's Jasper's dah," Issie says, straightening her shoulders and putting a little bounce in her step. "Stellan!" she calls out, loud enough that the man whistling stops as he appears from around the bend. He's tall and broad shouldered, an older version of Jasper.

Stellan opens an arm out wide and embraces Issie as she approaches. "What are you doing out here? Where's Ulissa?" He cranes his head farther along the path and spots me standing off to the side. "There you are. What are you two doing out here? You should be home, getting ready for tonight." His long, rich brown hair is tied low behind his head. That's the one thing that sets him apart from his son— Jasper has his mum's black hair.

Stellan releases Issie from his one-armed embrace while hitching up an enormous ax with his other. The edge of it is a bright silver, freshly sharpened and ready to sink deep into its next trunk. He stares at me, waiting for my answer. Behind my back, I clasp my fingers together nervously. "We're on our way home. Got a little distracted by the river and lost track of time."

"Ah, I see. Well, you two better hurry then." He moves past Issie, winks at me before continuing toward the forest. "I'll catch up with you two and your mum and dah later tonight."

Issie runs up to him, trying to keep pace with the towering man. Her legs stretch wide to match his normal pace. "And where are you going? It's a bit late for chopping wood."

Oh, my nosy sister. She can't ever leave Anumens alone to their business.

"Aye, it is. But Illia wants some fresh Umber bark to season tonight's dinner. Jasper snared his biggest river catch this afternoon." Stellan holds out his arm, toned muscles creating a bulge beneath his white shirt. "It's quite impressive. Possibly his longest fish yet!" He then hooks one thumb in the armhole of his leather vest before bending closer to Issie's face and suggesting, "You know, you and your family are more than welcome to join us for dinner. After we eat, we can all walk to the amphitheater together."

Issie has never been good at hiding her excitement when presented with an opportunity to socialize. Clapping, she hurries over to me. "Please, Uie! Please say you'll ask Mum when we get home!"

Ask Mum! Is she kidding? Mum is going to eat me alive when I get home.

Stellan's gaze follows Issie over to me. "Ulissa, make sure to send word to Illia either way. Come or don't, but we're happy to have the company." He shakes one finger at Isoldesse. "Don't linger. I'll be heading home soon enough."

Without another word, he twists away from us and continues on his way. He's out of sight in no time. Issie grabs my hands, tugging me out from the tall grass. "Come on-come on! We need to hurry! It's been ages since I've had one of Illia's to-die-for fish dinners! And it's Jasper's biggest fish ever!"

I give up on trying to keep my right foot clean and keep pace with Issie's brisk walk. She isn't wrong about Illia's fish seasoning. It's one of the most delicious things I've ever eaten that wasn't considered a sweet treat. The recipe is a secret, of course, and whenever someone asks what ingredients she uses, she'll say, "*My mum would come to me from the Unforeseen World and haunt me if I tell you. She'll howl in my ear morning, day, and night about how I've betrayed and broken a long-kept family secret. So nah, I will not be subjected to her haunting.*" Illia is a bit of an actress, so her response always comes with some theatrics, and a playful wink.

I'm not sure at what point our arms begin pumping at our sides, or when our brisk walk escalates into a *who could walk faster* game. Eventually, we end up jogging while playfully nudging one another. It feels good to momentarily forget what's waiting for me at home. I don't even mind my bare foot stepping in the occasional mudhole. It wouldn't be the first time I've come home with muddy feet, but it will be the first time I've come home after ruining a brand-new pair of boots. Oddly, the concern of getting yelled at doesn't weigh on me as much as before, and I suspect it might have something to do with seeing Jasper.

5

Issie hasn't stopped talking since we parted ways with Stellan. I don't mind. I never do. I'm not one to lead a conversation or purposefully join one unless required. Unless, of course, I'm venting to Jasper about you know who. Those moments on the grassy hilltop above his parents' home, away from Mum's earshot, are when I often dominate the conversation. Otherwise, I like to think of myself as more of a listener or an observer. I've never been one to enjoy hearing my own voice. But Mum and Issie, those two can talk and talk for hours. Anytime either has an opportunity to socialize with others, they seize it.

When we emerge from the forest, the path we've been walking parts in two directions. Going left will take us to the roundabout, which circles the village. Issie takes the lead, skipping along the right path, toward our farmhouse. The packed dirt ends, becoming a narrow strip of low grass that trails up the hillside of our pasture. We're almost home. Situated on the other side of the hill is one of the Red Umber Forest's largest clearings and our farm.

I move closer to my sister, leaning on her for support while I inspect my boot. I assume her silence is because she's watching me balance on one foot. "It's not ruined, which is good, and I don't think Mum will suspect anything if I tell her I misplaced the other boot. For now, at least." While I slide the boot back on my foot, I struggle to hold the one-legged stance and grab her arm for support. She doesn't protest or shove me away. Come to think of it, she isn't laughing or commenting on my plan to avoid getting into trouble. I regain my balance and ask, "What's wrong with you?"

Issie points a finger to the sky. I follow her gaze up the side of the pasture until I see thick black smoke billowing over the curve of the hilltop. There's only one place all that smoke can be coming from.

"Is that our—"

Isoldesse is running before I can finish. I take off after her. Though she's much faster than me, I force my jog into a sprint up the grassy hilltop. When I reach the top of the mound, our farmhouse comes into view below. Smoke is pouring out from the kitchen window, and even more streams up and out from the ventilation hole in the roof. The hole is as wide as I am when I spread my arms, and I silently pray to the Eilimintachs that the bundles of thatch canopying the ventilation hole don't catch fire.

I spot Issie at the bottom of the hill, ducking between the rails of our wooden fence. She's inside the house before I've reached the fence.

Oh, Mum, please be okay. Please, please!

I duck between the same two wooden rails Issie did before sprinting to the front door. I ignore my burning lungs as I push their limits for the second time today. The wooden door slams hard into the wall as I race inside.

"Mum! Mum, are you okay?"

Issie calls out from the kitchen, "Hold the front door open!" I can't see her as the kitchen is a separate hub from the main house, connected by a short hall. It's hard to refrain from running to her and checking on Mum, but I do as Issie asks. The second I swing the front door all the way open, a powerful current of air blows in from outside. My hands slip from the wood as the wind rushes at me, throwing me back. Thank goodness our sofa is nearby; otherwise, I might've landed hard on the wooden planks of our floor. The wind swirls once around the main living area of our home before streaming toward the kitchen. I stand and follow the river of wind down the hall. Loose tendrils of black hair whip my cheeks, and once inside the kitchen, I step out from within the current. One of Issie's arms is outstretched toward the open window above the sink while the other is commanding the wind to circle the room, collecting the fire and smoke from the stovetop, and leading it out the window.

Once everything settles and most of the smoke has dissipated, Issie releases her amula. Her voice is winded as she says, *"Déanta."*

"Thank the Eilimintachs you two showed up when you did!" Dah steps out from behind the long wooden prep table. His face, neck, and tunic front are covered in a thin layer of dark gray soot. His lips part and reveal bright white teeth. When his brown eyes meet mine, he erupts into a boisterous laughing fit. He shakes his head, and a cloud of ash floats up and into the air around us.

"What happened? And where's Mum?" I ask, stepping closer, unsure whether to laugh or cry at the mess.

"And," Issie adds, "why are you home so early from the market?"

Dah holds his hands out, glancing them over before picking up one of Mum's dishcloths. He carefully turns on the sink faucet, wets the end of the rag, and gently dabs the undersides of his fingers. "Market closed early today. When I got home, your mum mentioned you two were out playing by the river and that I should walk you both to the theater after dinner. In her rush to leave, she explained how to reheat the leftovers in the icebox, but it was said in one long breath. I barely understood what she was saying. Oh, how I wish your mum would ease up on always rushing about."

I hold Dah's wrist and lift his hand. No signs of blisters, but his skin is pink and slightly swollen. "Dah," I say while grabbing one of Mum's healing salves from inside the lower cabinet of an old hutch, "why didn't you wait for us?"

I untwist the wooden lid and scoop out a small amount of Mum's special healing concoction, specifically made for burns, then gently apply a thick coat to the underside of my dah's fingers. At first, he winces, but soon smiles as the sweet berry fragrance reaches our noses. Mum says it's important to add blurberries to the salve. It helps distract the patient from the pain of the burn.

"And where did Mum go?" Issie asks while handing me a ball of rolled-up linen strips. I gently wipe most of the salve from Dah's fingers, his light-brown skin now tinted a dark blue. The blurberries may have a sweet scent, but they'll leave your skin stained blue for days.

I wrap his fingers as he explains, "She wanted to be there when the Prinor family and Fawness arrived at the amphitheater."

Of course she did. It shouldn't surprise me she'd want to be there. I bet she doesn't even let Gunthrii get two words in.

Oh, Mum. She wants all the glory of a village's Adamant but none of the responsibility. She's happy to let poor old Gunthrii do that work.

On the bright side, Mum isn't home to notice or question why I'm only wearing one boot. Dah hasn't noticed, or he doesn't say if he does. After I finish wrapping his hand with the strips of linen cloth, he turns to the long wooden table and begins collecting the wooden bowls. Some are charred worse than my poor boot. "I should clean this mess before we leave. Don't want your mum seeing what I've done."

He knows as much as I do not to anger Mum. Poor Dah. "What were you trying to do?" I ask, returning the salve to the hutch. Mum's spice jars on the table are all salvageable and only need a quick wipe with a clean cloth. It's the black residue above and on the stovetop, along with the scorch marks on the corner of the prep table, that Mum will definitely notice.

"I thought I would help and prepare dinner for you girls before we head out tonight." He pushes one of the bowls on the table, trying to pick it up, but knocks it over instead. Issie's quick to catch the bowl before it falls to the floor. Dah thanks her and adds, "I may have overestimated my cooking abilities."

Only Dah could take a bad situation and bring humor to it. I often wonder how our parents have stayed together for so long. They are complete opposites in every way.

"Dah, you should've waited for us to return. We could've helped," I tell him, and retrieve a broom resting against a tall bookcase that stores our cutlery, dishes, glasses, tea sets, and flower vases. I sweep up the fallen soot into a neat pile.

Dah reaches over and holds the top of the broom. "Never mind your mum. She means well for you girls. But I am curious"—he raises his thick, bushy eyebrows and gestures with a nod to my bare foot—"what happened to your other boot?"

I never get nervous or tongue-tied when talking to Dah. No need to lie or stutter my words in fear of what he might think of me. "I slipped on the grass along the embankment and my foot landed in the river. I tried to dry—"

"We… We tried to dry it," Issie cuts in. "It was an accident. We were racing to the stone bridge."

"Ah, I see." The corner of his lips curls up.

"I messed up the amula. *We* were trying to draw out the water, dry the boot, but I messed up and now my brand-new boot looks similar to your dinner." Issie giggles while I continue explaining how we buried the boot.

"Oh, and we ran into Stellan on our way home," Issie adds, shifting the conversation to Stellan's dinner invitation. She finishes wiping the last of the ash from around the stove and approaches Dah and me. "Jasper caught his biggest fish, and Stellan invited us to eat with them tonight."

"Is that so?" Dah smiles. "And that must mean Illia's cooking her famous seasoned fish dinner. How delightful!"

"Yes!" Issie exclaims and returns to rinsing the rags in the sink. She tosses them into the dirty pile by the hallway and pleads with Dah. "Can we go? Please? Stellan said we can all walk to the amphitheater together afterward."

"I suppose so. It sounds as if there will be enough for all of us. But you'll have to hurry and get ready. No dillydallying," Dah says, specifically looking at Issie. "Ulissa, please send word to Illia that we'd love to come for dinner while I clean up." He pats his round belly, then pinches the tunic shirt while shaking his head. "I should probably throw this one outside and wash it myself tomorrow. No good will come if I mix it in with Mum's dirty clothes." He turns and heads out toward the main living, muttering, "I'll never hear the end of that if I ruin Talia's garments."

Issie races past me, shouting something about going to get ready. I make my way outside and over to one of our fruit trees. I pluck a leaf from one of the low branches and press it to my lips. This is one of those amulas I can do in my sleep. Softly, I say the ancient words, "*Ompar et focah doa* Illia." The small green leaf quivers against my lips—the signal that the amula has taken effect—and I speak the message meant for Illia with clear words: "Iya, Illia. We met Stellan in the forest and he invited us to dine with your family tonight. I'm sending word that we'd love to come and enjoy your famous seasoned fish dinner before the show. Thank you, and see you soon, Ulissa."

When the leaf stills, I hold it up high over my head and release it into the air. A gust of wind scoops it up and carries it off toward Jasper's home. As the leaf rolls in the wind, I can see the faint shimmers of light flowing through the leaf's veins, holding my message within its essence.

Once I can no longer see the small leaf, I hobble back inside and head straight to our bedroom. Issie is already there, selecting a new outfit to wear. I smile and walk past her to our private bathing room, where I close the door and begin undressing, piling my dirty clothes on top of the boot. I should've left it outside, but I'm still unsure of what to do with it.

I silently thank the Eilimintachs for the turn of events. Though Dah will probably get yelled at for the mess in the kitchen, I at least have avoided being locked away. A thrill of excitement surges through me— I will finally get to hear one of Fawness's magical stories.

6

ANOTHER MESS

Within twenty minutes, I'm wearing a lightweight green dress that hits just below my knees. It's sleeveless with a round neckline, and perfect for showing off my favorite necklace. Another gift from Daramum during my coming-of-age ceremony, where I transitioned out of the youthling phase and into the preadolescent, youthen stage of my life. It was an exciting time for me. I felt older, more responsible. As a youthen I could start my amula training at school and apply for an apprenticeship. Two things I'd been longing to do, mainly because they got me out of the house.

I think Daramum was even more excited about my transition than I was. She stayed an extra month longer than normal, which Issie and I loved. Mum, not so much. But during her stay, she gave me a special gift—an arcstone necklace. I knew the stone's purpose was to hold the essence of an Anumen once their physical life was over, that's if they chose ascension rather than continue on to the Unforeseen World. I also knew that the golden-yellow stones weren't abundantly available, so not every Anumen was offered ascension. The only one who didn't understand why Daramum gave me an unoccupied arcstone was Mum.

The slender stone of the necklace, which is about the length of my smallest finger, hangs at the end of a silver chain and rests above the curve of my dress's neckline. The golden-yellow color complements my light-brown skin, and I'm hoping it adds the right amount of glamour to catch a certain someone's eye. I know we're already going to be walking to the amphitheater together, but I'm hoping Jasper will pick up on my subtle hints that my feelings for him are evolving.

It's too early to confess how I feel because I'm not sure what I would do if I told him and he didn't feel the same. Our friendship would be ruined, and that's something I'm not willing to risk. Not yet, at least.

My thoughts are disrupted when a ball of fabric hits me in the back of my head.

"Hey!" I turn and gather a crumpled-up garment lying at my feet, then shake out the dress before draping it over my arm. My sister is waist deep rummaging through her wardrobe, still in her undergarments.

"Issie, why aren't you dressed yet?"

She momentarily withdraws from her search, and I gasp at her hair. Her braid is undone and gathered into a messy knot high on her head with a red ribbon.

I reel in my frustration and calmly say, "Issie, we really must get going." Everyone knows Illia isn't one to be kept waiting, especially when cooking.

Issie ignores me and continues huffing and muttering to herself. She parts two dresses in the wardrobe, squeezes between them, and digs through whatever she's got stashed in the back. During her search, I glimpse the Creator mark permanently inked between her shoulder blades.

It's a simple mark—an outline of a circle, and means she'll never bear youthlings. But it also means she has more power when casting amulas. That's the part Mum is proud of. Not many daughters are born

Creators, so for her to bring one into the world boosted her already swollen ego. Mum supposedly has big plans for Issie. I'm sure she has plans for me too, but I doubt my future will have anything to do with her plans to change Anuminis. She'll keep me locked up here at home with Dah for as long as she can.

That day I was marked as a Bearer, with the outline of a crescent on my back, was the same day Daramum gave me this arcstone necklace. I lift the yellow stone from around my neck and twist it between two fingers. She told me, "*You're entering a new stage of your life—a new awareness—and I know you'll do great things one day. I was given this arcstone as a gift, and since I have no use for it, I'm passing it on to you.*"

I know how powerful and rare arcstones are, and I tried to refuse it, but she insisted. She was adamant and explained that she has no intention of sticking around after her physical life ends. Being cooped up inside a magic stone isn't how she wants to live her second life. She wants her essence to be free—to live among the others who've passed on to the Unforeseen World. "*I always felt my purpose was best served here and now. You can decide when you're an old lady like me if you wish to ascend into the arcstone or pass it on to your darayouthens, as I am doing with you.*"

I let the stone drop from my fingers and dodge to the right when another crumpled-up dress flies by my head. Enough is enough, and we need to get going. "Issie! Just pick out a dress and let's go. You're going to make us late!"

"I can't find… Oh, where is it? I want to wear that shawl Mum gave me last season." Issie runs her fingers through her dark hair, pulling at the ribbon holding her hair up. The ribbon floats to the floor and her long black hair spills over her shoulders, covering the Creator mark.

"Issie, forget the shawl. What you need is to put on a dress! Dah is waiting!"

"What I need is to look my best for Fawness!" Issie yells as she wiggles her way between her hanging dresses to reach the back of the wardrobe. I glance around our room. I can't make out what's what from the mess she's created. There are piles of clothes everywhere. Shades of red, orange, yellow, green, and brown—all the colors that represent our region.

With one bare foot high in the air, the top half of her body swallowed up between hanging dresses, Issie shouts a muffled, "Ah-ha! I found it!"

"Great, now hurry so we can go."

She slides out from inside the wardrobe, dragging a mid-length burgundy dress in one hand and a pale pink shawl in the other. Issie shuffles through the mess scattered along the hardwood, over to our mirror. She holds up the dress and shawl against her body and admires her reflection. "Oh, yes! Fawness will certainly notice me in this dress. I just know it!" She spins and faces me. "What do you think?"

"I'm thinking you need to clean up this mess."

Issie's got her dress up and over her head, muttering words I can't hear from inside the garment. When her head emerges, she says, "I thought you said we're in a rush."

"Issie, you always do this! Why am I always the one to clean up your mess? Seriously, it's getting old." I crouch and pick up the shirts, shorts, skirts, and dresses closest to me. I find it absolutely ridiculous that Issie, Mum's pride and joy, is such a messy Anumen.

Issie finishes tightening and tying the ribbon trailing up the side of her bodice at the same time I finish cleaning the mess on the floor. I dump the pile in my arms onto her bed before slipping on my old leather flats. Of course, I would've preferred my new boots, but I'm stuck with these old things. They're tight against my toes, but I don't complain. I'll happily deal with sore feet tomorrow as long as I get to hear Fawness's story tonight.

With one hand on the wooden doorframe, I say to Issie, "I'll be outside with Dah."

She mutters, with her red ribbon pinched between her lips, "Ah-ha. Be out in a sec."

Outside, I see Dah by the fence overlooking our pasture. His arms are outstretched along the top railing and his gaze is angled up to the forest trees beyond our farm.

I rest my elbows on the top railing, and we wait for Issie in silence.

Without breaking his gaze, he says, "I wish your mum could appreciate the beauty of what we have."

Dah rarely speaks to me about Mum this way. Only after she's scolded me or punished me does he sneak in words of comfort. Something must weigh heavy on his mind, so I ask, "You think one day she'll find what she's looking for? Something better than this?"

The sun has set behind the treetops of the Red Umber Forest. A few moments later, I notice a floating leaf swirling in the wind, drifting down the hilltop toward me. I hold my hand out and the leaf gently lands in the center. Dah watches me as I press the leaf to my lips and recite, "*Liida focah oo ompar.*"

The message embedded within the essence of the Ittum leaf narrates in my mind: *"Iya, Ulissa. Stellan has returned, and dinner will be ready shortly. Happy to have your company. See you soon."*

Dah waits until I open my eyes to say, "Illia?" I nod and he adds, "We mustn't keep them waiting. Go and get—"

"I'm ready!" Issie sings as she dances out the front door, leaving it wide open. "We should get going. Illia's fish dinner will be the perfect start to a spectacular evening!"

Issie skips ahead, while I shuffle to close the door. Dah waits for me, and soon we're walking side by side toward Stellan and Illia's home. He's wearing a polished brown leather vest with a clean white tunic underneath that's tucked into his pants. As old as Dah is, he's held up his health well over the years. I may not be as content as he is with his choice of partner, but I hope to live a long and happy life—a *simple* life—here in the Red Umber Forest.

7

Stellan and Illia's home isn't too far of a walk. Most of the villagers' homes are built around the village center. A few, like those of our Adamant and our Healer, are located inside the village. And like most villages throughout Anuminis, our population is a fraction of that of the grandburgs.

Dah is walking with Issie. She clutches his arm and drags him into whatever story she's telling him. I let myself fall behind, admiring the serene sounds and natural beauty of the forest. Whenever she glances behind and waves for me to hurry, I point to my flats and wince, reminding her I'm wearing shoes that are too small and don't allow me to walk any faster.

It's partially true—my toes do hurt—but it's a subtle reminder that all my hard work to stay on Mum's good side and avoid getting into any trouble has paid off. I'll be on my way to see Fawness and hear her tell one of her magnificent stories after dinner.

When I get a whiff of Illia's fish seasoning, the savory aroma makes my stomach grumble. The herbs and spices are potent but not so overwhelming that I feel as if I might sneeze. Illia's a master at adding just the right amount of seasoning. The air smells delicious, and I can't wait to fill my belly.

Ignoring the tightness in my shoes, I jog up to Dah on the opposite side of Issie. "I hope Illia isn't upset that we're a bit late."

"I'm sure we're right on time." He nudges my arm with his elbow.

The forest breaks and we step out into a clearing. The path takes a wide curve, leading us around the base of an enormous grassy hill. On the backside, Stellan and Illia's home, burrowed into the side, comes into view. Lush grass frames the front of their home and trails all the way to the top of the hill, and for a moment I want to run up there and plant myself in the soft grass. It's where Jasper and I go to get away from our parents. Not that Stellan and Illia are anything like what I've got to deal with at my home, but Jasper has his frustrations with his parents. I love being up there with him. It's as if we're the only two Anumens on Anuminis. We laugh and talk during the day and watch the stars at night. I imagine he's up there now, waiting for me.

"Uie, hurry!" Issie shouts, returning my focus to the path we're traveling.

I look up and spot the stone chimney, about halfway up the hillside. A continuous trail of white smoke streams out, filling the air with a delicious scent. As we get closer, I see Stellan sitting beneath their wood pergola which provides shade to their outdoor eating area. He's sitting at the head of a long table made from red umber wood, holding a book in one hand and a metal mug in the other. When he sees Issie running toward him, he stands to greet her. Dah extends one arm out and they grasp each other's forearms, exchanging boisterous hellos.

"I'll help Illia," Issie says, skipping through the front door.

At the edge of the pergola, I lean against one of the large support posts. It pleases me to see Dah smile and engage in conversation without worrying about how his opinions will be received. I know I cherish moments in which I can be myself. Free to say whatever comes to mind.

"Iya, Ulissa," Stellan says, shaking me from my thoughts. He cocks his head with a grin, pointing to the path that continues across the front of their home and out toward the forest. "Jasper's checking his traps by the river, and I think Illia's about done. Go and fetch the boy. His mum will want him to wash up before we eat."

I push off the post and nod. I know exactly where Jasper's traps are because I helped him set them out yesterday after school. I leave Dah and Stellan to their conversation and head toward the forest opening. This stretch of the forest isn't like any other part of the Red Umber region. Stellan's dah planted Ittum trees long ago, creating a small wooded area filled with slender brown trunks and vibrant green bushels thick with Ittum leaves. It's one of my favorite places to walk, as it makes me feel like I've ventured out into a new land.

Looking up, I see clusters of green leaves, each leaf holding a green Ittum flower at its base.

The path leads me deeper into the forest. When I finally spot Jasper by the creek, I slow, hoping to sneak up on him. He's on his knees, leaning over the river's edge, fiddling with one of his traps. His back is to me, and if I'm quiet enough, I can surprise him.

For a split second I think I've got him, but then he says, "You really are the worst at sneaking up on Anumens." He sits up, rests one wet hand on his pants, and faces me. His head dips, and I can tell he's looking me over. "Well, you clean up nice."

Heat builds beneath my cheeks. I cross my arms over my chest and smirk. I feel like an idiot. But then I remind myself that it's only Jasper, my best friend for as long as I can remember. "What, this old thing? I guess. I wanted to dress up for Fawness."

"Yes, I can see that." He resumes working on his trap. I move closer, lifting the bottom of my dress and kneeling on my bare knees. I sit quietly and watch his hands work, which at some point had changed from lanky and frail to rough and scruffy. All part of the youthen transition. I changed a few years ago as well. Jasper poked fun at the new curves of my body that I was growing into. He lost the squeak in his voice while I lost some of the energy in mine. Our years as youthlings are a thing of the past and we are both moving forward through our youthen years, and before we know it, we'll be adults. Oh, how I can't wait to be an adult and make my own decisions. It's an exhilarating thought, yet oddly, I'm not in a rush to do it. As much as I dislike living at home, I am by no means ready to leave and live on my own.

Jasper curses while shaking his hand as if something has pinched him. I slap his shoulder. "Language."

"Sorry, but this fishing line isn't cooperating."

"Here, let me try." I scoot closer, pushing him to move and let me have a go at fixing his trap. He stands and lets me. I reach my hands down into the cold water and feel for the metal latch of the snare trap. When I find it, I loop the thin pliable string through the end of the snare and tie a knot. Running my fingers up the fishing line to check the tension, I feel multiple knots along the string.

"That should be good for now. The trap door will stay open unless your line breaks again." I stand and dry my hands with the underside of my dress, hoping any water marks will dry before we leave for the amphitheater.

"Thanks, Uie. And I know. I'm planning to trade for some new line next time Dah heads to Umberwood."

"Stellan's taking you to Umberwood?"

Jasper's face lights up. "I know, right? I'm excited too."

Cutting down the trees is one thing, but traveling with Stellan into a grandburg to help him trade the lumber means Jasper's doing well at his apprenticeship.

"That's wonderful, Jasper. You'll get to see the many sites of a grandburg."

"You mean Umberwood? It's not as big as other regions' grandburgs."

"But still," I say, dreaming of what it must be like to visit one of the larger communities. So many Anumens and so many places to explore. "You'll get to eat at fancy restaurants and browse all kinds of shops."

"I highly doubt we'll go to any fancy restaurants, and any shopping we do will be outside in the traders' markets."

"But still, the market circles the entire Umberwood borders. You'll have to come back and tell me about all the different vendors, and what they're trading and where they come from."

"Well, you're of age. Maybe your…" His voice trails off as he considers his words. "Maybe Tya will take you one day. You should ask her. Tell her it would be a good experience to visit Umberwood's amphitheater."

Oh, that would be amazing—to travel to Umberwood with Tya.

"Well, I think you and I know that's not going to happen. Not without *you know who's* permission, and there's no way she'd let me go anywhere like that without her blessing. But one can dream, I suppose."

"Uie, you'll be free soon enough. We're getting older and eventually, we'll be out of our parents' homes. I feel it in my gut." He comes closer and wraps one arm around my shoulder. He's a full head taller than me now. But I don't mind looking up. I don't think I'll ever *not* want to look at him.

"You feel it in your gut, huh?" I poke him in the side, wiggling my finger and tickling him.

He pushes away, laughing. "Stop it! You know that's a sensitive spot!" He collects his tools and stores them in a leather satchel, then slings the satchel over his shoulder before turning to me again. "What's wrong? Why are you staring at me like that?"

Mudals! Was I staring?

I blink several times and clear my throat. "I wasn't staring."

"Ah, yes you were. You were staring at me and… and smiling." His lips part and a mischievous grin spreads on his face. "Uie, what were you thinking about?"

Like I'd tell him! Though, it would be nice to tell him. Then I could be done with this internal torment of, *should we stay friends or make a go at being something more?*

"Dinner!" I blurt out. "Your dah sent me to get you for dinner."

His black hair hangs low over his brows. Only when he tilts his head do I see his rich brown eyes. Beautiful eyes that I could stare into for—

"Seriously, Uie. What's up with you today?"

I was staring again. "Nothing. Just nervous and excited for tonight, that's all."

We're about to leave and head back when he stops me with a gentle grab of my arm. His hands are cool from the river water. I follow him over to a wild-looking blurberry bush. I pluck one of the berries and pop it into my mouth. *Mmm, delicious.* "What's wrong?" I whisper.

He parts the branches and leans over the top, trying to get a closer look at something chirping from inside. "Uie, look."

I lean past his shoulder and see a small sparren hopping about in a pile of dry dirt at the base of the bush. It has somehow gotten caught beneath the tangle of thin branches woven over one another.

"It's just a youthling," he says and reaches down with one hand. The small creature flaps its wings, violently banging against the vine-like branches of the berry bush. "I can't reach it. The branches are too intertwined. Can you do something?"

My mind races to this morning with my boot and how I messed up that amula. "I don't know. My luck with casting hasn't been on my side today."

He withdraws from the bush, and we step away. With one hand on my shoulder, he tells me, "You're just as talented as the others in our class. Stop doubting yourself and you'll stop messing up."

"Oh, thanks. That makes me feel a whole lot better."

"*Uie*." He drags out my nickname. "You know what I mean."

He's right, of course. I think way too much when casting amulas and always second-guess myself, but I can't help it. I've been conditioned to worry and think about my consequences before I've even done anything. Unless I'm with Jasper. He always makes time to work with me—to help me get better at casting. Lately, he's been helping me with calming exercises to help clear my mind.

My mind is still turning over thoughts about my capabilities when I feel his hand slide from my shoulder, along my arm, and into my hand. He gently squeezes and says, "You know, I can tell when you're deep in thought. Don't overthink it. Focus on the sparren and how you're helping it. You can do this."

"But what if I hurt the little thing?"

He steps closer. My heart pounds inside my chest. He lifts my chin with his other hand, and our eyes meet. "Uie, all you have to do is take your time. My mum says the key to casting isn't about memorization, but about feeling the connection between you and the Eilimintachs. Embrace their presence." I narrow my eyes at him, because that's nothing like what the teachers tell us during our amula classes. He picks up on my questioning look and then adds, "Something like that. I don't know, casting amulas is your thing, not mine. Though, it would be pretty amazing if Anumen men could cast."

"Trust me, it's not as fun as you'd think. But I get what you're saying. I think I'd miss not being able to cast amulas." I move closer to the blurberry bush, and Jasper parts the top section of branches for me. The tiny creature is still stuck, flapping its wings and bouncing from one wiry branch to another.

Feel the connection, Ulissa. Feel the connection. I tell myself this a few times, mentally preparing while hoping I don't hurt the dear creature. I lean in closer, close my eyes, and focus on freeing the sparren. I don't think about anything else.

And then it happens. I see it in my mind, as if it's happening right before me though it hasn't happened yet—the branches parting, allowing the creature to fly free. The words I need to control the essence within the bush form in my mind. Words I've never known or heard before, yet, feel right. I've never felt this confident, and when I speak there's no hesitation in my voice. "*Oscii amach ag teacht troh.*" *Open outward and make passable*, I silently recite after I've finished speaking the amula.

Below, the thin branches of the bush quiver. The creature stills. Its tiny chest heaves while its black eyes watch from beneath the entanglement. Soon, multiple branches begin to slide over one another, drawing away from the sparren until a large gap emerges. The creature's body is trembling while it hops from one clawed talon to the other. It's only when I say, "You're free, little one," that it spreads its wings and flies free from its cage. I twist my body and move out of the way as the sparren bursts from the bush into the fresh air of the forest.

"I knew you could do it, Uie."

I look at the gap in the branches and say, "*Déanta,*" releasing the amula from its command. The branches spring back to their original crisscross pattern. When I straighten, I glance up to see if the sparren is nearby, but it's long gone, enjoying its newfound freedom. A freedom I long to share.

✹ ✧ ✹ ✧ ✹

We slowly make our way back to Jasper's home in the hill. The entire time, I'm still trying to understand what just happened. How an amula I've never learned in school came to me. Illia's advice to feel the connection worked. It was an amazing feeling, and I can't stop smiling.

As if he can read my thoughts, Jasper says, "I've heard of women who have a direct connection to the Eilimintachs. Besides Fawness, I mean. It's rare, but it does exist, Uie." He's trying to make sense of what I told him. I have no idea how that amula came to me, and when it did, I could feel it was the right words to say.

"You're talking about Sèaras. I'm not a Sèara."

Jasper stops and steps in front of me. "No, not like the Sĕaras. That's something entirely different. No one knows where the Sĕaras get their abilities of premonition. What you did back there was more in line with what Fawness can do."

"Maybe," I say and move past him. "I've never felt anything like it, so I can't say for sure." Jasper hurries to walk by my side, shoulder to shoulder as I continue, "I can't explain it, but it felt as if someone or something was showing me what to do and what to say."

"Amazing!" Jasper excitedly whispers. "You are truly amazing, Uie."

I come to an abrupt stop, dirt skidding beneath my flats. When he eventually realizes I've stopped, he spins to face me. His wavy black hair is pushed to one side of his forehead, and his tool satchel is slung over one shoulder. It's at this moment I realize I need to tell him how I feel. To tell him that my heart belongs to him.

The words are on the tip of my tongue when Stellan walks up from behind Jasper. He wraps one arm around his son. "Come and tell the story about how you caught tonight's dinner. I tried, but you tell it so much better than your old dah."

The two of them walk under the pergola and toward my dah where he sits at the table. The moment has passed, yet my mind hasn't changed. Today is the day I tell Jasper how I feel.

I'll get him alone sometime tonight and confess my feelings.

For a split second I wonder where this newfound courage comes from, but I like it. I silently pray to the Eilimintachs that this new feeling stays with me, encouraging me to do things I wouldn't normally do. Like telling Jasper how I feel or maybe even standing up to Mum. Though, I might be pushing my luck with that last one.

8

After Illia's delicious dinner, Issie and I help clean up before we all head out together along the roundabout path circling the outer edge of our village. The amphitheater is on the outskirts of our village, but on the other side from Stellan and Illia's house in the hill. The roundabout is the main path everyone travels when not needing to go into the village's center.

Large Red Umber trees line the gravel path, their thick branches sprouting crimson leaves and reaching out over us, creating a natural tunnel-like canopy.

Illia and Issie are walking and talking in the front of our procession. Dah and Stellan are discussing market trades ahead of Jasper and me. We walk slower to gain some distance from the others.

Dusk has set in, and I can see a group of Groundskeepers ahead, lighting the glass orbs staked along the path, illuminating the way. If my apprenticeship at the amphitheater had been denied by Tya, I would've liked to put in an apprenticeship request with the women of the Groundskeepers. Mum's always saying that *"the Groundskeeper position is a mundane occupation and only encourages this ridiculous simple life we're forced to live."* And by *simple*, she means one without technology.

The courage building inside has me feeling as if I can stand up for myself if the occasion calls for it. I feel as if I could scream in her face and tell her exactly what's on my mind, which excites me and scares me at the same time.

"What's turning inside that brain of yours?" Jasper shoves his elbow playfully into mine. He's changed out of his forest clothes and into a clean deep-red shirt with three wooden buttons along the left side of his collar. His shirt is neatly tucked into his brown pants. The same brown pants that he wore to our neighbor's marital union last season. I remember them because he sat in yellow frosting after one youthling left their cake on the stump he'd been sitting on. I don't know how Jasper missed seeing it there, but he sat in it.

"I was thinking how well you clean up too," I say, playing off of the compliment he paid me earlier.

He twists, showing me the backside of his pants. "Mum wasn't able to completely remove the frosting stain, but it's good enough that I don't think anyone will notice."

My eyes look at his backside, but only briefly. It isn't right to think about those parts of his body. Not yet at least.

I loop my arm through his and tug him forward. "Come on, we're falling behind."

We continue in silence. When we pass two of the Groundskeeper women tending to a broken orb, we slow to watch. One holds the cracked orb while the other mends the glass with an amula. They then relight the light inside. There is nothing mundane about their responsibilities, and honestly, I probably only know a fraction of what those responsibilities are.

We're about halfway to the amphitheater when Jasper leans closer to my face and whispers, "Uie, can we meet up after the show? I want to show you something."

Meet after the show? Is he serious? Show me something? What could he possibly want to show me?

"You know I'm not allowed to leave the house after dark. Not unless my parents are close by. Mum will lock me in my room with a containment amula for a week if I get caught sneaking out."

The others in our party round the bend, leaving Jasper and me alone. He doesn't let me walk on and clutches both my hands in his. I take a small step toward him, and he shuffles even closer. I lift my gaze and look up into his eyes. I don't know what he wants to show me, but I feel now is my opportunity to tell him how I feel. I part my lips, ready to confess, when a group of youthlings charge out from the forest behind him. They're yelling and waving sticks in the air, coming straight for us. We step back, away from one another, just as our neighbor's youthling, Augus, runs between us.

"Stop dillydallying, you two, and hurry up! Fawness isn't going to wait on you two kissy-faces!" He puckers his lips and mimics a kissing sound before spinning and running off with his friends.

"Kissy-faces?" I repeat, then face Jasper. He's taken a few steps back. His gaze is on the ground, and his hands are tucked into his pants pockets.

When he finally looks up, he says, "We should get going. Augus is right—we don't want to be late. You've been waiting so long for tonight I'd hate to be the one who ruins it for you."

He's too sweet, always so considerate. I desperately want to find that moment again, to say what's weighing on my mind, but he's right that we should get going. We slowly begin walking again, arm in arm. I offer him a smile, and he returns the gesture.

"Jasper." He doesn't look my way but squeezes my arm as if to say, '*Yes, I'm listening*'. Before I lose my courage, I tell him, "I'll find a way to sneak out and meet you in our spot."

His muscles relax beneath my hand, and his eyes find mine. "Really? You sure?"

I nod. "Though, I can't make any promises because if I get caught, then you probably won't see me until next season." I laugh and so does he, yet deep down we both know it's not a laughing matter. "But I'll try."

"Okay. I can't wait to show you what I've found."

Wait, he really wants to show me something. Maybe I'm reading his gestures all wrong?

"You found something. What is it?" I'll admit, he has my curiosity piqued. But I also know when Jasper has a secret, there's no prying it from his lips.

"I'll show you later. You won't regret sneaking out. Plus…" He swallows before continuing. "There's something I want to ask you. But later, okay?"

My entire body is tingling with joy and eagerness. It'll be the perfect ending to a perfect day. I can feel it. Or at least, I hope.

9

THE AMPHITHEATER

When we round the corner, gravel crunches beneath our shoes and I see a crowd forming at the intersection ahead. The road that crosses the path leads to the northern entrance of our village. Once we reach the crowd and head down the road, the amphitheater will come into view. I could walk this path blindfolded because I travel it every day to apprentice with Tya, Caretaker of the amphitheater.

"Jasper," I quietly ask, "do you ever think about where you'd like to build your future home? You know, the one you and your wife will raise your family in."

The corner of Jasper's lips curls. "My dah's already got plans to hollow out the other side of the hill for me and my future family."

I slow to a stop. "And you're fine with that? Living so close to them?"

"I am." His smile fades and his next words are drawn out as if he's nervous about asking. "I know you want to move away from… you know… your mum… but you don't plan on leaving the village, right? I'd hate to lose my best friend."

And there it is. How could I have thought we'd be anything more? He sees me only as his best friend. The confidence that I've been riding the last hour or so sinks, leaving my nerves cowering in a dark ditch of doubt.

I start walking again, passing him, and say, "I'm not sure what I want anymore."

We catch up to the others. Illia is off talking to some other women while Dah and Stellan are talking with a group of men. Augus and the other youthlings that almost trampled Jasper and me are nowhere in sight. I'm going to assume they've wiggled their way between everyone chattering outside to get front-row seats inside the amphitheater.

Our village theater may be smaller in scale compared to other amphitheaters, but it's definitely the most beautiful. There's nothing simple about it as thick Red Umber trees circle the enormous hole dug deep into the forest's ground. The theater's history was one of the first things I learned after I started training here.

Between the trees are thick vines covered in a vibrant green moss, and yellow flowers as big as my head have sprouted randomly along the exterior of the amphitheater. The only section not covered in them is the front entrance, a wide gap between two trees. Red branches crisscross overhead, and any gaps are filled with bushels of reddish-purple leaves.

I spot Issie talking with some friends from school. When she sees us, she excuses herself and makes her way over. Her burgundy dress and my dark green one coordinate with all the other Anumen women and girls wearing their best dresses. I love how amiable and happy the village is when we all come together. I only wish Mum would feel the same.

"How is Mabel?" I'm about to list off and ask about her other friends when she pulls both me and Jasper off to a secluded part of the path. I can tell by the bounce in her step that she's eager to include us in whatever news she's discovered. "What is it? What's happened?"

"Oh, Uie!" Issie waves us to come closer and we do. "Mabel has just told me the most exciting news!" Issie draws us into a huddle. "Mabel heard from Nella, who heard from Ester, who overheard while browsing the bakery shelves, Gunthrii telling Padda that Fawness is planning on picking someone from the audience to bring up on stage to help tell her story!" Issie's eyes are as big as the yellow flowers decorating the outside of the amphitheater. "How exciting is that?"

"Why would Gunthrii tell Padda that?" I question, crossing my arms. "I'm not saying Ester's wrong. I'm just saying Padda is our village baker and has nothing to do with what goes on at the theater. I would've thought that's something to discuss with the Caretaker of the theater."

"I don't know why, and who cares," Issie snaps. "He said it, and Ester overheard it."

"At the bakery?" Jasper doesn't sound convinced either.

"Yes, at the bakery." Issie gives us an eye roll, unswayed by our questioning glares.

"Ester snoops too much. You really should—"

My sister is quick to cut me off. "She's not lying! She knows what she heard!" Issie marches past us. "Be that way if you must, but I'm going to try and get a seat as close to the stage as I can, even if that means sitting with the youthlings!"

We watch her stomp off. Jasper tells me, "I'm not sure I'd trust Ester's word. The girl has a habit of stretching the truth."

I nod as Mabel, Nella, and Ester hurry inside after Issie.

"We should head in," Jasper says, and I follow him through the dwindling crowd to the front entrance.

I'm always in awe whenever I step into the amphitheater, which is every day since I'm an apprentice here. But it never gets old. It's a wondrous construct that was built generations ago and still stands strong, thanks to the line of Caretakers like Tya. Which I'm proud to one day be a part of.

Inside, Jasper and I stand on the entrance landing. It's not a large space, but enough for fifteen or sixteen Anumens to occupy comfortably. I can't help but notice how much dirt has been shuffled inside over the beautiful red planks. I make a mental note to sweep these floors first thing tomorrow when I come for my shift.

Ten paces in, a staircase descends from the center of the audience seating. There's a railing that lines the top, preventing anyone from falling down. It's made of vines the width of my arm, twisted into a long rope and then molded into a sturdy railing that curves along the top foyer area.

As we step farther underground, an earthy smell fills the arena. Narrow rows of bench seating form a semicircle in front of the stage. The walls along the sides of the theater are padded flat and decorated with green, brown, and yellow banners. Each banner has a red tree embroidered at the end, representing our Red Umber Forest region.

About halfway down the stairs, I see Tya on the stage. She's lighting the glass orbs lining its front. She's too focused on casting illumination amulas to notice me and it's too loud for me to call out to her, but still, it's nice to see her.

Each step is a large red plank embedded into the dirt, forming the column of stairs. I spot Augus and his friends climbing over one another in the first and second rows. Having youthlings of my own isn't too far off in my future, and that scares me a little. I don't want to raise mine as our mum raised Issie and me, yet I'm not sure I know any other way.

Behind Augus and his friends are Issie and her friends. They're as front and center as she'd hoped. Me, I'm just happy to be sitting next to Jasper. He turns and shuffles along a fairly empty row and sits next to his friend Braum. I follow, taking the seat next to Jasper. Braum waves a hello to us both and then, before either of us can ask him how he's doing, Braum tells Jasper about some wild creature he caught out by the northwest corner of the forest. Jasper twists and listens.

I turn my attention to the stage again, where Tya is adjusting the pale blue curtains hanging toward the rear of the stage. The curtains are held up by heavy wooden beams that extend from one side of the theater to the other. Behind them is the backstage area. Our beloved Fawness is back there in the dressing room, getting ready. Or at least I hope she's back there.

It isn't until I spot my mum standing on the stage, off to the right, that my excitement dies a little.

All that matters is that I'm here, and there's no way she can send me home.

10

I sit quietly, half listening to Jasper and Braum and half watching Mum below. She's talking with a group of women I assume to be a part of the Prinor family. Gunthrii stands near Mum. Though, he's facing the crowd, smiling and waving as everyone takes their seats. He looks to be close enough to be included in the conversation, but not so close that he's imposing on Mum's space.

Smart man.

Gunthrii glances over at the Prinor women every few minutes, but mainly focuses his attention on the Anumens entering and taking their seats. He's a portly man, who Mum always says sweats too much. He waves and nods and smiles and plays the part of our Adamant well.

He catches me staring and offers me a sympathetic nod. I wave back, knowing exactly how he must feel. He's the official Adamant of our village, and here our mum has dismissed him as if *she* were the Adamant.

My gaze wanders over to the two older Prinor women standing opposite my mum. I would say they both look about the same age as her, but their beautiful dresses give them a more youthful glow. Their skirts are layers of white and light-blue sheer fabric, billowing out from beneath the hems of their bodices. The layers drape all the way to the stage floor. Their bodices are fitted and cover their arms all the way down to their wrists. Smooth, silky-looking fabric—a luxury I'll never experience in my lifetime.

Three Prinor youthlings wearing knee-length dresses stand in front of the two women. The first and tallest of them is in a pale blue dress while the youthling in the center wears a soft yellow. The farthest, and presumably the youngest, has a muted green dress on. I'm not sure if it's because green is part of our region's colors, but it's my favorite out of the three. All the youthlings have the same braided hairstyle with colorful flowers, each coordinating with the colors of their outfit.

I jump in my seat when Issie calls my name and slides next to me. She grabs my hand and tugs. "Mum keeps looking over here. I think she wants us."

The second she says *Mum*, I look across the stage to where Mum is standing, hoping her back is still facing the arena seating, but it's not. She's looking directly at us, her brown eyes glaring in our direction. She's wearing one of her nicer dresses. One she saves for occasions like tonight. It's long, a deep purple color with a scooping neckline. The sleeves end at her elbows and are fitted like the rest of her dress. It's only the skirt portion that billows away from her body. She waves an impatient *come here* in our direction.

I highly doubt Mum wants to see me.

I pull my hand free from Issie's. "I'm sure she's only requesting you, Issie. There's no reason for me to come." I pray to the Eilimintachs that Issie gives in and hurries along without me, but she doesn't. She only tugs harder.

"Nope. You're coming with me. This is the perfect opportunity for Mum to introduce both her daughters."

"Issie," I say with a somber, pleading tone while trying to remain seated, but she's persistent in her tugs, and I start to think that keeping Mum waiting will only anger her even more. Regardless of whom she's really wanting. My arms go limp in defeat, and I stand. "Okay, let's get this over with."

Issie's shuffling down the row toward the stairs while I turn and tell Jasper I'll be right back. He's sweet, and asks, "Do you want me to come with you?"

"Better not, but thanks."

I slowly follow, descending the steps toward the stage. Issie rushes ahead, the distance between us spreading wider with each passing second. She reaches Mum before I get a foot up on the stage. My stomach pinches and my nerves tingle beneath my skin. I can't imagine what Mum will do to me if I throw up Illia's fish dinner in front of the Prinor family.

I linger behind the group of women. Mum has her arm draped over Issie's shoulders, drawing her close. There's another woman, someone I didn't notice before, standing across from Mum. I sidestep to get a better look at the old woman. Her fine white hair is loosely tied up and away from her face, and the blue cloak wrapping her shoulders is so dark I almost believe it to be black. She doesn't appear interested in the group discussion as she leans against her staff and stares up at the night sky. The polished wood of her staff has a beautiful swirling pattern of light and dark wood. The lower half tapers to the ground while the section above the old woman's hands is covered in dents and divots, twisting into a round knot at the top.

It's only when the youthling in the muted green dress waves a small hand to me that Issie looks over her shoulder, then back to the youthling and says, "That's my older sister, Ulissa."

Mum briefly turns. Her smile flattens and her eyes narrow, but she's quick to face the Prinor women again and resume their conversation, ignoring me altogether.

"Who is this delightful young Anumen lady?" A shaky voice cuts through my mum's mid-sentence.

The round knot of the old woman's staff points straight at me, and then she uses it to push my mum aside. Mum's expression tightens. Even if no one else can see it, I know there's fire rising inside her right now. "Oh," she grits her teeth while saying, "this is my eldest child, Ulissa." She steps closer to me, eyes telling me to go away. "What do you need, dear?" The word *dear* sounds forced.

But I'm not the only one who catches the hidden venom in Mum's voice. Issie's got one hand over her face. She spreads her fingers just enough to look at me, dread glossing over her eyes. She mouths the words *I'm sorry* before snapping her fingers shut to hide from the mess she's brought about.

Your sorrys *aren't going to help me now.* I narrow my gaze, mentally scolding my sister. I should've listened to my instincts and stayed with Jasper.

"Uh…" I stammer. I want to explode. To stand up for myself and show Mum that I have value. That I'm a part of her family too. But I don't. Fear has me locked into a stare with her. "I was looking… for, uh…" I need to give her an answer that will get me out of here quickly and keep her from yelling at me later. My brain screams for my mouth and tongue to move. *Say Tya. Tell them you were looking for Tya!* After a long pause, I manage to spit out, "Tya. I was looking for Tya."

Mum's eyes ease from their narrow glare. Saying I'm looking for Tya is believable enough. She points to the opposite side of the stage where Tya is now talking to Gunthrii. Her gaze drifts up and down my appearance and stops at my feet.

Time to leave.

I take a step backward, ready to return to my seat when something hard hits the stage floor. It's the old woman's staff. She's walking toward me. Each hit of her staff is louder than the previous. "Now, wait a moment," she says, a slight pitch to her voice as she drags out her words. "Don't run off just yet. Come, come. Let me get a better look at you." She beckons for me to meet her halfway.

I resist the urge to look at Mum. I don't need her permission, but I've been conditioned to get it regardless. I take two steps closer. I'm a head taller than the old woman, so I can't help but to look down at her. The dark cloak she's wearing is pinned together by an oval white stone brooch. The stone is as smooth as her staff, and the old woman notices me staring. Her frail fingers move up and touch it. Wooden bangles, all different colors, rattle around her wrist. That's when I notice the four bracelets on her other wrist. They're not made of wood. Instead, one is black stone, another appears to be made from bone, the third is a metal that has an aged patina to it, and the last is a strange braided bracelet made from what looks like thick green vines.

"You wear eight bangles," I say, glancing over her wrists.

She rests her staff against her chest and holds out her hands. "Yes, one for each region."

"Why?"

"Why not?" One of her eyebrows rises.

Mum snaps from behind the woman, "Ulissa, don't be rude. The Sėara doesn't have time for your ignorance."

A Sėara. An actual Sėara standing in front of me. Can she read my mind? I stare at the old woman and think, *I think I'm in love with my best friend.* I'm not sure why that thought popped into my mind to test the Sėara's ability, but she doesn't react to my mental proclamation.

"I'm sorry. I didn't realize—"

"Oh, stop that. No apologies necessary. How are you to know one old woman from the next." Her smile is inviting and friendly. "Tell me again, what was your name?"

"This is my—"

"I was asking the girl." The Sėara swings her staff out, blocking Mum from coming any closer or speaking any further. Mum backs away, offering a weak smile to the Prinor women.

When the Sėara draws her staff in and leans on it, I say, "Ulissa."

"Ah, yes. Ulissa. I remember now. I believe I've been waiting to meet you."

Hearing that a Sèara has been waiting to meet me is not what I was expecting her to say. The air around me suddenly feels as if I am standing directly beneath a sun beam. I pray to the Eilimintachs that I don't ruin my dress with the onslaught of sweat beading under my arms. I am about to question the woman's meaning when I remember that it's normal for her to have visions, or premonitions about Anumens. But why *me*?

"Is that so? I'm really a nobody."

The corner of her mouth curls up. Her brown eyes have a foggy sheen over them, yet I can tell this woman has so much life in her.

"Just because you think you're a nobody doesn't change the fact that you're somebody I've been destined to meet. You and your sister." The Sèara turns and beckons for Issie to come closer. She's hesitant and glances at Mum, who nods in approval. Mum stands nearby, hands nervously rubbing her arms while crossing her chest. I bet it's killing her not to be included in this conversation.

Issie moves to my side, each one of us holding one of the Sèara's hands. Her staff angles back, leaning against her body. "You two might not realize this, but you *both* have important roles to play in the future of Anuminis."

My sister and I shoot a quick look at one another. It isn't uncommon for a Sèara to speak in riddles, and from what I've heard, Sèaras aren't allowed to divulge specific details about their visions or premonitions. Not even to the Prinor family. Life must unfold as the Eilimintachs intend.

"What does that mean—important roles?" Mum tries to wiggle her way into the conversation. "Both girls? Are you sure?"

The Sèara gives Mum an annoyed side glance before saying to Issie and me, "I see two futures for you girls. One leads to disappointment and regret, while the other leads to strength and new beginnings." She tightens her grip on my hand, her bony fingers cool against my skin. "But one fate cannot happen without the other."

The evening air turns thick with tension. I let the Sėara's unclear words sink in while Mum begins to list off questions that ironically form in my mind as well.

"Which future belongs to which girl?" There's an authoritative demand in her tone that surprises me.

Has *she* forgotten who she's speaking to?

The cheeks of Mum's light-brown skin flush, and her chest rises with every breath she's taking. She must be fuming.

Oh, this isn't going to end well.

Mum storms around the old woman and steps in front of Issie and me. She hunches over so she's eye level with the Sėara. "Never mind about which future belongs to which—I don't need *you* to tell me which of my daughters holds greatness. But I would like an explanation as to what you mean when you say *new beginnings*. You mean the Old World ways? Is that the new beginnings you're talking about? Will Issie bring back technology?" Mum stands tall, straightening her shoulders. She gestures with a narrowed look to the women of the Prinor family standing close behind the Sėara. "I demand an explanation. You need to command her to reveal her meaning."

Before any of the women in fancy dresses can answer, the Sėara holds the rounded end of her staff out toward Mum. "When was the last time an Anumen commanded another Anumen? I believe it was during your Old World days, Talia."

The Sėara moves past Mum with a slight limp in her walk and calls Issie and me to come again. When we approach, she removes two of her bangles and hands one to each of us. "A token to remember this moment."

We each take note of the other's gift. Issie holds one of the Sėara's wooden bangles. It's a polished piece of red wood, representing our region. The black bangle I hold is also polished but it's cold like stone. It's not black like a starless sky, but more like a dark, smoky black with hints of faint gray veins. I know exactly which region this bangle represents. Though, I don't understand why the Sėara gave it to me, and I can't bring myself to say the region's name, not even silently in my head.

Of course, the bracelet I want was given to my sister.

"Thank you," we say in unison, except there's a little more pep in Issie's gratitude. I'm still trying to piece together the Sėara's forewarning and the bangles she's given us.

The old woman's wrinkles crease around her eyes as she offers a small smile. "This is only our first encounter. Though, I cannot say our next encounter will be as pleasant." Before either of us, or Mum, can respond, a tall man with long black hair tied behind his head approaches, leans down, and cups his hand to the Sėara's ear. "Yes, of course. I will see to it before Fawness takes the stage. Come, come." Without another word, the man escorts the Sėara off the stage and carefully up the center steps toward the entryway. Everyone moves from their path, giving her space to walk.

Issie slips her hand through the reddish-brown polished wooden bracelet while I clutch the smooth black stone of my bangle. Tears build behind my eyes, but now isn't the time to cry.

"Take your seat, girls," Mum says, and as Issie hurries to her seat with her friends, Mum is quick and grabs my arm before I move. She drags me past the Prinor women and youthlings as they too move off the stage, taking their seats for the show. She's turned so her back faces the crowd; that way, no one will see the look of anger on her face.

"What were you thinking? Why would you interrupt me in front of the Prinors like that?"

"Issie said you wanted to see both of us," is what I want to say, but what comes out of my mouth is, "I thought you were waving to both of us."

"Why on Anuminis would I call for you?" She takes hold of my wrist and examines the bangle. "This is a sign meant to help *me* decide your future." When she releases my hand, I hold the bracelet to my dress. In her usual cold tone, she says, "We'll talk more at home after the show." Then she exits the stage, leaving me to stand there in front of everyone, trying to rein in my tears.

Through blurry eyes, I look at the black bangle. Mum's words float through my mind: *"This is a sign meant to help me decide your future."*

Why does she always make things about her? Why can't she just accept me and trust me to live my own life?

I can't hold back the tears, and I'm not ready to return to my seat, especially when I'm upset. So instead, I spin and run off to hide backstage.

11

I don't want to think about my or Issie's future anymore. I just want to be left alone. Alone—maybe that's the only way I'll find happiness. In solitude.

I duck under and around a few stage pulleys and ropes hanging from the beam above. There's a long wooden bench along the wall at the far end of the blue stage curtain and I sit. It's not quiet, since there's only a curtain separating me from the commotion of the audience, but it's private enough.

Most of the backstage area is underground and split into two levels. Tya has only lit the glass orbs closest to the stage, leaving the lower section in darkness.

I'd be tempted to make a run for it if there were an emergency exit, but then again, I've worked so hard to get here. No. I'm not going to let her ruin my night. I'm going to enjoy Fawness's story.

I can smell the earthy scent from the thick roots dangling from the trees above. I touch the arcstone hanging from my neck. If Daramum were here she'd know exactly what to say. With no one around, I slip off my shoes and stretch my toes. Mum wouldn't be too happy with me walking around barefoot, but my toes ache and the fresh air feels amazing on my feet. But I don't care. Anger swells inside me because who is she to decide *my* future?

"Why am I such a coward? Why can't I say what's on my mind?"

"Ulissa? Is that you?" Tya's voice comes from the dark shadows in the lower level of the backstage area. Her voice is muffled behind the yellow curtain of the dressing room. Fingers appear, pulling open the edge of the curtain. She steps out and quickly drags the fabric along a railing, closing off the doorway. My curiosity is piqued, and I wonder if Fawness is back there getting ready.

My mentor walks up the three steps to where I'm sitting. She notices my bare feet but says nothing. Instead, she asks, "Why aren't you in your seat?"

"Oh, well… I needed a minute away from— I mean, I just needed a minute to myself." Jasper is the only one who truly knows how much crap I deal with at home, but Tya's keen observations have always clued her in to what life must be like for anyone living with my mum. Plus, she's known my mum since they were youthlings.

Tya moves past me, over to a wooden crate filled with empty glass orbs. Lifting the box, she narrows her eyes at me. "Something you want to talk about?"

I shake my head.

"Good, because Fawness is about to take the stage and you need to be scooting along." That's when I realize Tya's not wearing her usual Caretaker frock. She's dressed in a simple brown sleeveless dress with tiny red flowers embroidered on it. A thin leather rope is wrapped twice around her neck and hangs low down the front of her dress. A small white stone the size of my thumbnail is attached to one of the ends. It's her transessent stone, which reminds me of the white stone brooch the Sèara was wearing. If that was a transessent stone too, then it's the largest one I've ever seen. The amount of power that thing must hold…

Tya's staring at me, and instead of leaving, I offer to help. I extend my hand to take the crate for her, but she shakes her head. "You'll get your pretty dress dirty. Besides, it's your night off. Go and enjoy the show."

"I will. But in a minute. Please."

Tya sets the box of glass orbs on the end of the bench and cocks her head. "Were you trying to get a sneak peek at Fawness? You should know better than that. But fine, a minute. Then to your seat."

I turn my head and stare at the yellow curtain to the dressing room. "Is she back there?"

When Tya doesn't answer right away, I turn and face her. But she's gone. The faded blue stage curtain sways in her absence.

I'm about to slip my shoes back on when I catch the strangest light refracting in the backstage lower level. No, not light—tiny plates of contorted mirrorlike shapes, and they're moving closer to me. I stand, watching the anomaly in front of me. Eventually, the refractions form the shape of an Anumen.

"Hello," I whisper while glancing over my shoulder at the stage curtain. I should probably run for help, but curiosity has gotten the best of me. It isn't long before the plates of refracted space dissipate, revealing a tall woman, probably the most beautiful one I've ever seen. The orbs behind me cast a gentle glow on the woman. Her dark hair is loose and drapes over the fronts of her shoulders, down her cream-colored dress. It's a short-sleeve dress with a curving neckline. The skirt is slightly full and falls below her knees. She steps closer, her dark brown eyes staring right at me.

"Where did you come from?" I ask, reaching one hand out to feel the empty air behind her. "And what was that?"

"That was a concealment amula. A little trick I taught myself when I need some alone time." The woman strides up the steps and sits on the bench. She pats the polished surface, gesturing for me to sit, and I do.

"Are you… Fawness?"

She nods.

This is happening to me—not Issie! Me! I'm sitting backstage with FAWNESS!

"H-how…" I stutter a bit, still in shock that I'm sitting next to the most powerful Anumen on Anuminis. "How did *you* create an amula? I thought only the Eilimintachs could *create* amulas."

A small bubble of laughter escapes between Fawness's lips. "It's not as easy as it sounds. And it's not something many can do."

"You can because you're Fawness, right?"

"Yes and no." Her gaze dips to the packed dirt floor. "Is there something wrong with your shoes?"

I lift the skirt of my dress and hold one foot up. "They're a bit tight. I would've worn my new boots but, well, let's just say it hasn't been a lucky day. But now I'm here, and I'm excited to hear you tell us one of your wonderful stories." I try to sound happy, but it's hard with the Sėara's words still twirling in my mind.

Fawness holds one hand out, palm upright. "Place your hand over mine and close your eyes. There's something I've been instructed to show you."

"Show me? By whom?"

"The Eilimintachs."

I hesitate, but only for a second. Being the Fawness means she's got a direct connection to the Eilimintachs. So, for her to say she has a message or something they want me to see is believable. I close my eyes and slip my hand over hers. Her skin is warm. No, wait… It's cool, and getting colder. I want to open my eyes but don't. Her other hand slides over my knuckles and she tells me, "Keep your eyes closed, Ulissa."

Fawness knows my name. This is insane!

Behind my closed lids, the world around me melts away. Darkness fades and an image forms in my mind. I see an old woman. At first, I think it's Daramum, but then I recognize the familiar lines of the woman's face and smile. It's me. I gasp and hear Fawness's voice in the distance. *"The Eilimintachs wanted to share a piece of your future life with you."*

"I look happy."

"Yes, you do," Fawness whispers.

The home I'm walking through isn't a farmhouse like ours or a house built inside the side of a hill, like Jasper's home. Instead, it's built up on the side of a mountain where the rocks are black, overlooking a village below. Inside, the walls are filled with photos of Anumens of all ages. One photo in particular shows me as an old woman sitting with a group of youthlings.

"Are those all my darayouthens?"

Fawness doesn't respond. The scene continues as the older me steps out onto the balcony of the home. It's nighttime and I'm alone, reading a book when someone steps out of the shadows and startles me. It's… It's Isoldesse, but older. She's wearing strange clothes. Fitted white pants and a long white coat. Her black hair is short, cut just below her ears and parted to one side. Older me smiles, yet she's crying, which confuses me. I watch as the older me's expression shifts from happiness to concern as Issie sits at the end of the lounge chair. It's almost as if they haven't seen one another in ages.

Issie speaks, but I can't hear what she's saying. "Why can't I hear her?" I say out loud, hoping Fawness will answer.

"Whatever you hear or see is all the choice of the Eilimintachs," Fawness says in my mind.

I focus on the vision again. Issie is holding the arcstone necklace Daramum gave me. Old me glances inside the house and then back at Isoldesse's hand, and asks, "Is that my—"

Issie cuts me off, saying, "Forgive me, dear sister…" Her words fade, as does the vision, until there's nothing but an infinite blackness like one would see when they close their eyes before sleep.

I blink several times before my sight returns and I'm looking at the backstage area again.

"What was that?" My hand slips from Fawness's and I hug it close to my body. "Why show me only a snippet of time, and so far in our future?"

"The Eilimintachs don't often ask me to be a conduit to another Anumen. But when they do, there usually isn't much explanation. What you saw may or may not be relevant to what the Sèara told you. You and your sister are connected, and our world is entangled by your actions."

Great. More riddles.

I jump to my feet, slip on my shoes, and cross my arms tighter around my stomach. "So, I'm supposed to live my life always questioning and thinking, *Will today be the day I disappoint the entire planet? Is today the day I will regret for the rest of my life?*"

Fawness remains silent and allows me to huff in frustration while pacing the small space. After a moment, she gestures to the audience waiting beyond the stage curtain. "I think it's time for me to go out there."

"What story are you planning to tell?"

She smiles before answering, "I want to show Anumens a story. To tell them the truth about why we live the way we live."

It's odd to hear the word *show* when someone's planning to tell a story, but who am I to question our Fawness.

I nod and am about to leave her to collect her thoughts in private when she opens her arms wide and gestures for me to come. I close the space between us and let her wrap them around me. There's a sweet aroma, like honey and blurberries, coming from her dress.

Her voice is soft as she whispers, "Do not live your life questioning yourself. Do not let others steer you to a life in a direction you don't want to live. You've seen a glimpse of your future. You know you grow old and will be surrounded by family who love you. Get to that point in your life before worrying about the Sèara's prophecy. I tell you this, but the message comes from the Eilimintachs."

"Thank you," I say, muffled against her long black hair. I step away and with one hand she urges me to go and take my seat.

My mind has never been more confused yet so clear about what I must do. I must break free of my mum's control. I lift the black stone bracelet and whisper, "My future ends up somewhere in the Black Mountain region."

12

The moment I sit in my seat next to Jasper, the orbs lighting the arena dim and darkness falls over the audience. Everyone's conversations drift into silence as we wait for Fawness to take the stage. Above, the stars twinkle as if waiting to hear tonight's story as well.

A few moments later, Tya opens the blue stage curtain to reveal Fawness, who's holding a glass orb, unlit, in the palm of her hand. She slowly moves forward, her gaze sweeping over the Anumens who've come to hear her tell one of her famous stories.

"Iya, villagers of the Red Umber Forest."

"Iya, Fawness Basira," everyone answers in unison.

"I'm honored to be here, and to share one of my stories with you. You may be familiar with this story, the origin of amulas, but I'd like to retell the tale."

I hear a few disappointed groans and subtle sighs, probably because every Anumen within the eight regions can recite this story in their sleep. The origin of amulas begins with the first arcstone, which was discovered in a cave deep within Black Mountain. Black Mountain was only a mountain back then. Not part of a region. The only region during the Old World times was on the other side of the planet, isolated from the rest of the world. Today that territory is known as the Unspoken Ninth Region. It's a forbidden territory that Mum has been trying to get to for as long as I can remember but her requests are continually denied by the Prinor family.

Though others are groaning, I'm curious because backstage Fawness had said, *"I want to* show *Anumens a story."*

Mum, off to my right and sitting three rows up with Dah, is still, her gaze glued to Fawness. I can't tell if she's excited because it is a story of the Old World ways, or if she's flustered like most Anumens around me.

"This should be good. I wonder what'll be different from her point of view," Jasper leans closer and whispers in my ear.

"I talked to her backstage and she said she's going to show us her story."

He twists, his knee smashing against mine. "You talked to Fawness? Just now? Backstage? And you're only telling your best friend this amazing piece of news now!"

"Sorry," I say with a blush. "It all happened so fast."

"Tonight. I want to hear all about it tonight, okay?"

I nod and he turns his attention back to the stage. Sneaking out tonight may not be happening, especially if Mum wants to discuss the conversation Issie and I had between us and the Sėara. But there's no need to dwell on maybes right now.

On stage, Fawness lifts her empty hand to her midsection. Streams of blue and white energies swirl up from her palm, arching across the front of her and into the glass orb in her other hand.

With a loud voice, she says, "I understand it's a story you've all heard. But you've never heard the story like the way I'm going to tell it—to show you."

"You were right," Jasper whispers. He lowers his hand to his side. His fingers graze mine. I flinch and turn to look at him, but he's watching Fawness. *It was nothing*, I tell myself and return my hand to my side. Our fingers barely touch. Fawness is moving from one side of the stage to the other, her cream-colored dress swaying at her knees. She's about to begin when I feel Jasper's finger hook over mine. My heart reacts and beats hard against the inside of my chest. This time, I don't look at him, but I do press my fingers closer to his. The silent gesture between us just might be the thing I needed to regain my courage and tell him how I feel.

I'll find a way to sneak out tonight. I look at the black bracelet on my wrist. There are other things I need to tell him before I confess my feelings.

"Do not be afraid," Fawness says, her voice amplifying up to the trees and out into the night sky. I'm no longer thinking about Jasper but listening to Fawness's instructions, as is everyone in the amphitheater. "If at any point during the story you wish to stop, close your eyes and count to ten." She glances down at the youthlings. "For you darlings, if you don't like what you see, then just close your eyes." Fawness provides a demonstration and squeezes her eyes shut before opening one and smiling. The youthlings in the first and second rows laugh.

"Before I begin, I would like to call on a volunteer to help me with my story."

Anumens young and old shout out and raise their hands, wanting Fawness to call on them.

"Settle down, settle down. Ulissa, could you please join me on the stage?"

Mum watches me with an utter look of disgust on her face while Dah's smile has never been wider. He's beaming with pride. I walk down the steps and up the stage to Fawness.

"Iya, Fawness," I say with a nod.

"Iya, Ulissa," she says while prompting me to stand center stage. There's a shadow over the audience and it's hard to make out their faces, but I find Issie and wave. She waves back. Her eyes are wide and elated to see me up on stage. Her smile gives me a boost of confidence.

"I need you to hold the orb," Fawness says to me and then continues to speak to the audience. "The energies inside the orb are two amulas that I'll be using in tonight's story. Remember, if you decide you don't want to participate, close your eyes and count to ten." She glances down to the youthlings and winks. They all wink back, or at least try. Augus is blinking both eyes and scrunching his nose with extreme effort.

"All right, let's begin. Everyone, listen to the sound of my voice." She inhales a deep breath and begins reciting, "*Eso oo fis lii Olahar radhac coo et olra.*"

I've never heard most of those amula words, but somehow my mind translates: *Show your vision by giving sight to the many.*

Inside the glass orb I'm holding, the blue and white energies merge, emitting a bright light that fills the entire amphitheater. The brilliance of the light doesn't hurt or make me want to close my eyes, but it does take over my vision. The amula takes hold and Fawness begins her story.

13

The night is gone, replaced by a beautiful sunny day. I'm alone, standing on a hilltop with nothing but green hills for miles.

How is this possible?

"Listen to my voice and let the story unfold before you. Just enjoy and watch," Fawness says with a softness that floats through my mind like the breeze that passes over me on this hilltop.

Without controlling my body, I'm turning to face the opposite direction. The view changes and I've never seen anything so magnificent in my life. In the distance are multiple columnar towers. The towers reach so high their angled tips slice through the drifting clouds. Sunlight reflects off the mirrorlike windows covering the exterior.

Below, at their base, are smaller towers that shoot up from the ground like a sea of pointy icicles. The smaller towers are everywhere and range in height.

My foot lifts to take a step down the hill and when it lands, I'm thrusted forward in a blur, transported to the grounds below the towers. The grass has vanished and is replaced with an endless amount of gray stone. Gardens with colorful flowers are sectioned off within the gray sea. My body moves forward, as if I'm walking around and sightseeing in this strange place.

"Welcome to the old world," Fawness says, appearing next to me.

"This is the Old World? It doesn't look scary at all."

"It's not the structures that cause fear, but the Anumens up there." Fawness points to the top of one of the tallest tower buildings.

"Is everyone seeing what I'm seeing?"

"Yes, and I'm telling them the same story I'm telling you."

I follow Fawness and we move up a grand set of stairs leading into one of the tall towers.

"There was nothing wrong with this world. It was a prosperous one with many advancements in technology, medicine, and community structure. They even had the ability to travel the stars." Fawness waves her hand in a circling motion, and we're taken farther inside the tower. It's a grand space, larger than anything I've ever seen. The floors are polished white and so smooth I can see myself looking back. Hundreds of Anumens walk every which way. Some float up on rising platforms through a glass tube, and some descend down other tubes. I can't believe this was our world once. It's overwhelming yet beautiful.

I step up onto one of the metal platforms and instantly I'm lifted into the air through one of the glass tunnels, up to the next level of the building. Fawness leads me toward a dark corridor at the back of the tower. I step inside, and the deeper I go, the darker it gets. When I emerge from the tunnel and out into the openness, I realize I'm back on the hillside where I started. It's nighttime and the stars are bright.

Something pulses a gleaming light among the stars. It's getting bigger and brighter. It changes from a white light to a golden yellow, then red before momentarily disappearing.

"What is that?" The object suddenly emerges like an explosion from within the clouds. "Is that a ship… from space?"

This time when Fawness speaks, it's in my mind. *"Our people were on the brink of making contact with another world, but the Eilimintachs felt that it wasn't our time to branch out. That's where our story begins."*

The hilltop stretches out before me, as if I'm flying up and up, and out beyond the skies until I'm looking at the planet from space.

"The grandburgs of our ancestors, those who lived in the Old World, remained in one isolated region, leaving the rest of Anuminis untouched." The planet spins to the opposite side, where Fawness illuminates the borders to the current eight regions. *"The beginning of our amula abilities comes from this side of our world. A land rarely visited during the times of the Old World."*

My body descends from high in the sky over the area we now call The Black Mountain Region. My stomach drops but only for a brief moment before I'm once again standing on solid ground. There's a lone mountain before me and I'm in awe at the view. I've heard stories from Daramum about the Black Mountain, but I've never traveled north to visit the region. Yet here I am, seeing it through Fawness's story. Everything feels so real. The cuts of the mountain are sharp and black, as the name suggests, but the rocks that form it are not shiny. Instead, there's a thin layer of sooty dirt covering the black surface, almost like dust that's collected on a forgotten piece of furniture.

Fawness continues her story. Her words are in sync with the scene unfolding before me.

"It's here that a young woman named Fawn came across a cave on the southern side of the Black Mountain. Inside, she traveled deeper and deeper, following tight tunnels and slippery slopes until she reached a small cavern. Exhausted, Fawn made camp. Lying awake on her blankets, she caught something glimmering a golden-yellow color high along the black wall of the cavern. With her knife, she wedged the stone free and the moment she closed her fingers over it, a bright

orange light casted out, filling the cavern. The light faded and our dear Fawn was passed out on the floor. It's here, while she slept, that the Eilimintachs were forming the very first bond between Anumen and arcstone.

"The Eilimintachs woke Fawn, but only her mind. Her body remained on the cavern floor, asleep. They introduced themselves and the power of amulas—to speak words that temporarily controlled the Eilimintachs around them. Fawn trained for years with the Eilimintachs, but when she woke on the cavern floor, only three days had passed.

"She tested her new abilities and called for light to lead her out of the cave. A ball of light appeared, and she followed it. The Eilimintachs had told Fawn that the moment their bond took effect, the dormant connections within all Anumen women were awakened. It was Fawn's responsibility to go out and teach others the words to use when casting amulas."

Fawn stands on the outskirts of the Anumen society. The angle of the scene moves in close and follows the first Fawness toward the sun-reflected towers.

"After a few months, when most Anumen women had grasped their new abilities, questions began to arise. Many saw amulas as a blessing, to help them in their everyday work, and were grateful to the Eilimintachs. But it was the Anumens who sought to better Anuminis with more technology—more advancements—by combining technology with the power of amulas that troubled the Eilimintachs.

"No matter how hard Fawn tried to convince those self-righteous Anumens living in the tops of the towers, they were set on their greedy ways. They ignored her warnings, which only angered the Eilimintachs even more."

The scene changes. I'm standing in an open room with white walls on one side and a crystal-clear glass wall bowing outward. When I glance through the window, the ground is nowhere to be seen. Only a layer of thick clouds, circling below.

"It was here, in this meeting room, that a group of Anumens decided they were going to travel the stars. And not only travel the stars, but try and rule them too."

A group of Anumens sit around a long oval table. The sleek tabletop is whiter than the clouds drifting outside. One woman, dressed in a white uniform, stands and speaks to a man sitting across from her. "You once said if we discovered a way to protect ourselves, exploration to other worlds could begin. Well, not only can we protect ourselves, but we can bring other worlds to their knees."

"Yes, I believe the Eilimintachs have provided us with exactly what we needed, and more." The man twists in his seat, facing the woman to his right. "What is the status of your training facility?"

The woman straightens her shoulders, eyes gleaming with satisfaction. "We're ready for occupancy. We'll begin recruiting youthen girls within the week."

I can't believe what I'm seeing and hearing. How can this be the same Anuminis? And how are we related to these Anumens? They're talking about building an army of youthen girls.

Fawness speaks in my mind, answering my unspoken questions. *"Training girls at a young age was easier than seeking out older ones. They wanted to build and command an unstoppable force of powerful women."*

The world around me spins in a whirlwind, transporting me outside to an open field. It's nighttime and off to the right, the towers stand bright with their lights in the distance. Out in the middle of the field is Fawn, her arms spread wide.

Fawness continues narrating. *"Negligence to listen angered the Eilimintachs, and using Fawn as a conduit, they acted. They couldn't allow amulas to be used as weapons. The power that flowed through Fawn that day has never been recreated. An immense amount of energy coursed through her veins and out into the world, causing a planet-wide blackout."*

Out in the field, Fawn releases waves of energy in every direction from her body. When the wave hits the towers, their lights flicker into darkness.

"The blackout lasted several weeks and set the Era of Chaos into motion. Tension erupted within the city. Anumens fought over how much power and knowledge was enough, and how they'd angered the Eilimintachs. Anumens living high in the towers tried to use their power to weaken their own kind into submission. It was all-out chaos."

I can't believe what I'm seeing as Fawness goes on telling the story. Anumens are fighting everywhere. They're arguing in the courtyards, acting out with graffiti, destroying the beautiful gardens, and casting amulas against one another. I've never seen such violence and aggression in our world.

Fawness speaks again as the scene unfolds. *"The Era of Chaos lasted fifty years. Some say it was a viral infection that caused Anumens to act out, to be aggressive and power hungry. Whatever the real reason, it was evident to the Prinor ruling family that they'd have to decide for the entire planet. Do they revert to simpler lives without technology or ask the Eilimintachs to take back their gift of casting amulas?"*

I swear I hear my mum gasp from somewhere out in the real world.

"After five decades of fighting, the Anumens, exhausted on both sides, made the unanimous decision to leave technology behind. To live simpler lives without the temptation to want more."

Daylight breaks and the scene shows thousands of Anumens in numerous processions traveling away from the towers. A darkness falls on the once-thriving city as Anumens come to stay in the new world regions. The new era shines a bright beam across my vision, restoring my sight in the process. I blink several times, as does everyone in the audience.

Fawness steps to the front edge of the stage, her back to me. "It may take a few seconds for the amula to completely wear off."

My eyes adjust and I'm staring out at the audience. Everyone is whispering and murmuring to their neighbor. Fawness turns and faces me. She takes the empty orb from my hands.

"Thank you for your help, Ulissa. Go ahead and take your seat." She gives me a gentle push.

I'm almost at my seat when I hear Fawness say, "It's an honor to be your Fawness. Being Fawness means a lot of responsibility to carry the knowledge of our history and bear the direct connection to the Eilimintachs. Fawn, the first Fawness, was also given another special gift that has been passed down from Fawness to Fawness. We are the only Anumens to be both a Carrier and a Bearer, but with only one seed. One seed to continue the Fawness line."

"Did you know that?" Jasper turns and asks.

I shake my head. "How can she be both? That's impossible."

"You are the luckiest Anumen in our village, you know that?" he whispers. "You got to talk with Fawness backstage, and you got picked to be her story helper."

Tonight did turn out pretty amazing. "Yeah, but *shh*. She's not done."

Fawness stands at the front of the stage, clutching the glass orb with both hands. "Thank you all for coming to hear, and *see*, my story. I hope you all have had a wonderful experience, and I look forward to coming to your village again." And with that, she retreats backstage while Tya closes the stage curtain. The audience bursts into cheers and applause. The orbs lining the walls and surrounding the amphitheater illuminate, lighting the arena.

"That was amazing!" Jasper turns to me, stretching his hands over his head. "It felt so real!"

"It did," I say, stretching my own arms and adding a yawn.

"You're tired?"

"A little."

"Oh," he says with a sad look. "Too tired to meet me on the hilltop?"

I smile and recall his fingers hooking mine. "I'll try but remember, no promises."

"I'll take it! If I don't see you, I'll know why." He gives my hand a quick squeeze, and then Braum is shaking his shoulders and drawing Jasper's attention away from me. "I'll catch you later," he says with a wink before following his friend up the amphitheater steps.

Issie is quick to hop into Jasper's seat. "That was amazing! And she picked *you*! What was it like being so close to Fawness? Did she say anything to you before she began? Oh, Uie, you have to tell me everything!"

"Come on, let's not keep Mum and Dah waiting. I'll tell you all about being on stage while we walk home." I don't plan on telling Issie about the moment backstage with Fawness. That's for me and me only. Well, me and Jasper. I have so much to tell him tonight. That's *if* I manage to sneak out.

14

The crowd walking the path that circles the outskirts of our village has thinned out. Anumens talking and recalling moments from the show have made their way to their homes. Now, it's just our family walking the path home. Issie and I are arm in arm a few paces behind Mum and Dah, who walk an arm's length apart. Unlike them, when I'm united with a husband, I plan on holding his hand or walking arm in arm all the time.

"Okay, now tell me. Mum's far enough ahead that she can't hear." Issie pulls me closer. She clutches her pink shawl, which is draped over her shoulders. The night air has cooled, and I wish I'd grabbed a shawl too.

"She told me to hold the glass orb, that's it."

"Ahh, you're so lucky. To be close to our Fawness."

"Issie, what do you think the Sėara meant?"

Issie makes a humming noise as if she's thinking about the moments that took place before the show. I twist the black bangle around my wrist. Will Mum send me away to the Black Mountain region? Or if not, should I make the decision to go on my own? Dah's sister lives in the Black Mountain region. I could stay with her. The Eilimintachs did show me that I would be living there, but that was later in my life. Maybe I'll eventually move there?

"I think we're too young to make big decisions like that." Issie's voice breaks my thoughts. "Best to let Mum read into the Sèara's riddles."

I stop, the gravel crunching beneath my shoes. "Are you serious? You'd let Mum decide your future for you?"

Issie smiles as if I've said something humorous. "Of course, silly. She's our mum. She may be strict, and she may have crazy dreams of bringing back the Old World ways, but you have to admit she's one of the smartest Anumens we know. I trust her opinion."

"Well, yeah, because she's always done right by you."

"And maybe if you stood up for yourself more, then you wouldn't think her opinion so negative. You're always trying to be someone you're not in front of her—to please her, but maybe you should start acting like you. Let her get to know you… the real you… and what you want. It's a two-way path, Uie, and you need to start opening up to her."

I'm absolutely floored to hear my sister tell me that I've basically failed at trying to talk to my mum. That I should work harder to have my voice heard. Is she crazy? Does she not know what would happen if I spoke out of place?

This is not the time to start an argument, only because Mum will hear, and I have no desire to bring Mum into an argument that will only end with me being locked in my room for the night. I have plans to sneak out.

I continue walking and Issie follows. We walk the rest of the way in silence. When we arrive home, the front door is open. Issie and I press our backs to the wall and listen. I only hear one voice, and she doesn't sound amused at all.

"You've never supported my ideas or projects," I hear Mum yell. Her voice is harsh yet pleading. "You used to believe in the Old World ways too. We used to work together in trying to convince the Prinors to allow us to travel to the ninth region."

"Talia, that was a long time ago. Long before Ulissa was born. Before we had this farm. You need to be here with us now, not off trying to bring back the past. Especially after what Fawness showed us tonight. How can you still be so sure it's the right thing to do?"

Issie and I are standing outside the front door, waiting for the right moment to go inside. I tilt my head to get a better angle to hear Mum's answer.

"She showed us what she wanted to show us, and nothing more. It's a story. A fictional story to keep Anumens in line. The Eilimintachs are trying to keep balance by creating some ridiculous story about a virus causing Anumens to go mad. How absurd is that? Even if it was real, we know better now. We can live a balanced life with both technology and amulas."

Before Dah can answer, Issie and I walk in. They both turn and face us. Mum looks us over, and her gaze lands on our wrists. "What took you so long?"

"We've been outside talking, just in the front yard." Issie closes the front door. The old farmhouse has seen better days, but it's a good home. I recall the home old me was living in when Fawness showed me that glimpse of my future. That was a well-taken-care-of home too. A place and a life that appears I was happy to live.

I silently thank my sister for trying to ease Mum's mood. I also pray that it works, but I'm guessing not even the Eilimintachs can extinguish the fire blazing inside her right now.

"Can you believe that nonsense? What gives her the right to spread such lies?" Mum has both hands on her hips. She hasn't changed out of her dress yet, and I glance over at Dah and he's still wearing his nice clothes too. Seeing Mum this worked up makes me nervous. I slowly move along the wall, toward the kitchen corridor. If I can make it over to our bedroom, then maybe I can say a quick goodnight and leave her to stew in her own anger. I don't want any of that anger to trickle over and find me.

But she catches me out of the corner of her eye and flicks her attention to me. "And I suppose you believe that slithering snake?" Mum steps closer, her finger firmly pointing at my face. "One good thing that came from that little performance was that we got to see how beautiful the old world was. Can you believe those amazing towers?" Mum tilts her head back, eyes to the ceiling as she clasps her hands in front of her face. "The grounds were meticulous, and the people all looked so clean in their white garments. It was the most inspiring sight."

Her moment of bliss is short lived, and then she's narrowing her eyes at me again. "Why should we pay for their mistakes? We should be allowed to try again. To bring back technology and continue exploring the stars. There's so much out there that we can learn from and that others can learn from us."

"Talia," Dah cuts in, "I think it's late. The girls need their rest."

Mum doesn't move. She holds her stare on me. Like she's waiting for me to agree with her. I can't help but think of Issie's words, *"You're always trying to be someone you're not in front of her—to please her, but maybe you should start acting like you."*

"I think the old world was beautiful, but it's our past. Not our future. If we want to keep the connection to the Eilimintachs and the use of amulas, then we mustn't go against the Eilimintachs." Saying exactly what's on my mind feels exhilarating, yet a nagging fear that I should've kept my mouth shut lingers. And when my mum steps closer, the heat in her cheeks spreading over her light brown skin, my arms tremble with anticipation of what's to come.

"You little traitor. You—" Mum starts, but Issie's between us in a flash.

"Mum, Ulissa has a right to her own opinion," my sister calmly explains. "Dah," she says, looking past Mum, "we're going to bed.

Good night." Issie grabs hold of my hand and pulls me toward our room.

"Oh, no you don't," Mum yells and grabs my arm, dragging me from Issie's side. "You know what I think. I think you need to start working on that disappointing future the Séara foresaw. That's what I think." Mum looks over to where Dah has stepped closer. "I think Ulissa should pay a visit to your sister out in the Black Mountain region." She faces me, fingers gripping tighter on my wrist, and with venom in her voice she says, "Permanently."

I swallow hard, holding back the tears that have long been waiting to come. I say the words I never thought I would actually say to her: "You don't want me here?"

"The Séara obviously wants you there."

Tears stream down my cheeks, and anger boils inside me. I narrow my eyes and yell, "You're just looking for any reason to get rid of me! You are the worst, and I wish the Prinor family would just let you go off to the ninth region. That's right! *You* should go! Not me—YOU!"

She stands there, motionless and staring at me with wide eyes. A single tear falls from her eye. "You worthless—"

"Talia, that's enough," Dah cuts in. He steps between us, and she's forced to release my wrist. She shoves him hard, trying to get him out of the way. No more talking—I can tell she's ready to put me in my place. Hands out, palms facing toward me, she's about to cast an amula that will whirl me into my room. And not in a gentle way. When I see her lips part, I know it's coming. Issie cries off to my side, and Dah is regaining his balance. It's not the first time she's gotten this angry and done something this aggressive toward me, but it's the first time I counteract.

With my own outstretched hand, I submit my mind to the Eilimintachs and let them empower my amula. Their energy comes swiftly and when I see Mum getting ready to speak her own amula, I yell with every bit of emotion I can, "*Ganea mise comlac*," and then I disappear.

15

Okay, so I don't completely disappear, but I do vanish from their ability to see me, just as Fawness had done backstage, which is odd because she never told me that amula *and* she'd created it herself. How did I know what to say? I stand there as amazed as Mum, Dah, and Issie. It's like looking through crackled glass.

Mum stumbles backward and Dah catches her. He studies the space where I stand, or where he last saw me stand.

"Where is she? How did she…?" Mum's voice cracks.

"I don't know," Dah mumbles.

I turn and see Issie, her eyes wide with her hands cupped over her mouth in shock. "Where did she go? Who taught her such a powerful amula?"

Mum steps closer, her hand swiping the empty air. I try moving out of the way, but I'm not fast enough and her hand passes through where I'm standing—right through my body. I can't help the yelp that escapes, and then quickly cover my mouth because I'm unsure if they can hear me. No one looks in my direction, so I assume my voice is also contained within the concealment amula. I tiptoe, just in case, as the three of them continue to investigate the spot where I cast the concealment amula.

Not wasting any more time, I hurry into my room because I'm not sure how long the amula will last. I climb out the back window of our bedroom and race toward the woods. It's too early to meet Jasper on the hill above his home, but I head in that direction anyway.

When I'm far enough from the house, I say, "*Déanta,*" and the concealment amula fades until the plates of distorted space are gone and everything looks normal. I pick up a stick and tap my arm with it. The stick doesn't pass through it, so I know I'm me again.

It's dark and I can't see. I know where I am, but I need light to see where I'm walking. I whisper, "*Tarach bach sola,*" and a small ball of light forms in front of me. It's one of the first amulas we're taught at school in case we ever get lost in the woods at night. I avoid the main path just in case there are any lingering Anumens from after the show, or in case Mum and Dah are out looking for me. When I break through the tree line along the back side of Jasper's home in the hill, I say, "*Déanta,*" and the ball of light swirls out of existence back into the night air.

At the top of the hill, Jasper's silhouette lies in the grass. He's there, even though it's earlier than the time we agreed on. The moon is high and surrounded by a black sky speckled with tiny white sparkling flecks. I kneel down next to him and ask, "How long have you been out here?" When I twist to lie next to him, I land closer than expected and my shoulder bumps his. He doesn't react and I don't move away.

"Oh, I came straight up here when we got home. I wanted to watch the stars."

I don't mention anything about what happened at the house. I want to put all that behind me and just be here with him.

"Anything exciting happening up there tonight?" I lift my chin to take in the stars to my north. Fawness said that our ancestors from the

Old World discovered a nearby world and considered making contact. That's crazy to think about—traveling the stars and visiting other worlds.

"I noticed something strange a few weeks ago. I think it's always been there. I've just never noticed it before." Jasper points up to a bright star off to our left. "That star over there never moves."

"You sure?"

"Yup. Ever since I noticed it, I come up here before bed and check to see and it *never* moves. The stars around it shift to the east every night, yet that star sticks to the night sky like a bug stuck in tree sap."

That is strange. I've never been one to study the stars or their movements. I know they move but only because our world spins around the sun. There's a lot of information about our world, including climate, terrain, and star maps, that was carried over from the Old World. That information was classified as important, and since most of the information had nothing to do with technology, the Prinor family transitioned the records to our new way of life when the Old World ways were cast aside.

"You should study the stars instead of following Stellan's line foraging trees for trade. You're too smart to be stuck here."

Jasper rolls onto his side, propping his head with one arm. I stare up at his face, which is outlined by the moonlight. I can barely make out the lines of his face, and what I do see appears to be a confused, furrowed look.

"I thought you said our life was here, in the Red Umber Forest?" He asks, brushing a lock of my hair from my forehead.

I can't help the smile that spreads from his touch, and the fact that he said *our* life was here. My smile fades as my earlier plan resurfaces in my mind. If I want to be free from my mum and her ways, I need to leave. I need to make my own future. It breaks my heart to leave Jasper here, and for a second, I choke back my words, thinking maybe tonight isn't the night to share what I've got planned. But he deserves to know. He's my best friend in the whole wide universe and I trust him more than I trust anyone. He's my support and anchor. He keeps me from falling into a depression of sorrow brought on by the Anumen who gave me life.

"I can't stay here." I twist the black bangle on my wrist.

His chin dips to his chest and he sighs. I can't imagine what he's thinking right now, and I'm not sure I want to know. I know he doesn't want me to leave, but I'm not sure if it's because he's losing his best friend or… I want it to be for the other reason, but I also don't want to get my hopes up.

"Where will you go?" he finally asks while raising his head.

"To live with my dah's sister"—I lift my wrist and twist the black stone bracelet on my arm—"in the Black Mountain region." She doesn't have a home on the mountainside like in the vision Fawness showed me, but maybe one day I will. Maybe this is the way I live out a happy life. The way I grow old and have youthlings of my own.

"When?"

"I don't know. I just know I need to go."

"What did the Sėara say to you? She must've said something to give you this courage. You're willing to leave the home you love—"

"I don't love my home. I love this village. I love apprenticing with Tya at the amphitheater. I love my dah. I love Issie, and I love…" I pause, realizing I'm about to include Jasper in this list.

He reaches over with his free hand and combs it through my hair, trailing his fingers along the side of my face. He leans closer, our lips inches from one another, and says, "I love you too," before closing the space between us, pressing his lips to mine. For a second, I'm caught off guard, but then I relax and drape my arms over his shoulders, pulling him closer. My fingers rake through his hair, and I'm doing everything I can to hold onto this moment.

He draws back, and whispers, "Where you go, I go."

I have no words or response, so I lift my head to his and kiss him again. My courage explodes inside my body, and I know with every ounce of my being that we're doing the right thing.

I choose to believe that my future isn't the one filled with disappointment, but rather with strength and new beginnings.

ACKNOWLEDGMENTS

The Red Umber Forest started out as a short story I'd written a few years ago. It was a writing exercise I did to help better understand some of the characters in Isoldesse. Dusting it off the shelf, I decided it would be a good companion novella between books one and two of the Aevo Compendium series.

Thank you to my beta readers Meghalee and Chasity for providing me with reader feedback to help tighten the story flow. I'd also like to thank Kelly Harper for her beta reading feedback and line edits. A story cannot evolve without beta readers, so thank you.

A shout out to Liz Delton for helping fine tune the blurb's book description. Liz has been a wonderful writer friend, helping me with industry questions and writing advice during my self-publishing journey. To many, many more years of friendship! Thank you, Liz!

Next, I cannot thank Nikki Mentges from NAM Editorial enough for all her hard work in editing this story. Her line edits, story suggestions, and resource references go beyond my expectations, and her attention to detail was amazing. Nikki was amazing in double checking the titles and terminology used in this novella to Isoldesse, making sure the two were cohesive. Thank you again, Nikki, for all your hard work.

I'd also like to thank my biggest supporters—my family. My husband, Jim and our three daughters, Kayla, Abby, and Chloe, have always cheered me on and encouraged me to keep going. I'm beyond blessed to be able to write while doing the wife and mom gig. I love you all to the moon and back.

ABOUT THE AUTHOR

Kimberly Grymes lives outside the Wichita, Kansas area with her husband, three kids, and two miniature pinschers, Jubilee and Cori.

She recently released her debut novel, ISOLDESSE book one in the Aevo Compendium duology series. Since then, she's been busy writing short stories, this novella, book two of the Aevo Compendium series, and dabbling with writing a middle grade story.

www.KimberlyGrymes.com

Follow Kimberly Grymes online:

Instagram: @KGrymes.writes

Twitter: @KimberlyGrymes

Facebook.com/AuthorKimberlyGrymes

Be sure to use tags when posting
#KimberlyGrymes #TheRedUmberForest